The Cake Man

The Cake Man

Gregory Dixon

www.urbanbooks.net

Urban Books
1199 Straight Path
West Babylon, NY 11704

ISBN-13: 978-1-933967-84-4
ISBN-10: 1-933967-84-6

First Printing April 2009
Printed in the United States of America

10 9 8 7 6 5 4 3 2 1

This is a work of fiction. Any references or similarities to actual events, real people, living, or dead, or to real locales are intended to give the novel a sense of reality. Any similarity in other names, characters, places, and incidents is entirely coincidental.

Distributed by Kensington Publishing Corp.
Submit Wholesale Orders to:
Kensington Publishing Corp.
C/O Penguin Group (USA) Inc.
Attention: Order Processing
405 Murray Hill Parkway
East Rutherford, NJ 07073-2316
Phone: 1-800-526-0275
Fax: 1-800-227-9604

Dedication

This book is dedicated to Paulette, who is my physical, spiritual, and emotional center. Thank you for keeping me focused on the work to be done. You are the inspiration that gives me the confidence and courage necessary to overcome the obstacles that keep me away from the keyboard. Thanks. Sugar.

Acknowledgments

The list of people who contributed to making this work possible is long, and full of people who really cared about and encouraged me in the work. Paulette, Lisha, Andrea, Andre, Tina, Mama, Al Hatter, everyone at the camp, Vic, and the whole family. Of course, the engine that drives it all is my friend, agent, confidant, chief critic, and biggest fan—Linda Williams. Words cannot express all this beautiful lady has done for me. Thanks to you all, and especially to Carl Weber and his entire organization, for making the dream a reality.

The Cake Man

Prologue

"What the fuck do you mean we got jacked?!" Big George King literally shook with rage. He bent and picked up a stone flowerpot near the fireplace where he was standing and hurled it clear across the room. As pieces of stone, dirt, and plants scattered, the two street dealers in the room cowered and backed toward the door.

Boar Hog just stood patiently and waited for his boss to collect himself, as George's nineteen-year-old son Chris watched silently from the patio.

"I mean that some niggas from Studewood hit the house on Yale. Technically, it's in their hood, not The Four-Four, but you already knew that."

When George got angry, his Mississippi roots started to show in his speech, though it had been decades since he'd left the little country town in which he was born to come to Houston. "Them muthafuckas had to know whose shit they was fuckin' wit'." He looked his old friend in the eye. "I want to know everything there is to know about the dumb asshole behind this shit. Get Fred, Moochie, an' the twins from Bethune together, but don't do nothing yet. I'm gonna go with you."

Chris stepped into the room. "I want to help, Daddy. I'll go with you."

George whirled to face his only son. He realized that the boy only had to look up a little to meet his eyes. Big George King stood 6-2 and weighed nearly 300 pounds, none of it fat. Although he did spend time in the health club these days, his hugely muscled arms, legs, and chest were gifts of nature. The gym only defined and amplified them.

Anger drained away from his face as he looked at Chris. "You know damn well that ain't gonna happen, Chris. I know you as down as they come. I know you can shoot with the best of them, really shoot an' not just spray bullets. An' I know you got heart. Shit, you been following me around since you could walk. Come month after next, though, you goin' to college. You're gonna learn to take this money I make and turn it legit, as well as multiply it. That's been the plan since the day you was born, an' ain't nothin' changed."

Chris saw the set look on his father's face and knew it would be useless to argue. As much as he worshiped his father, he wasn't going to oppose him. He gathered his car keys and left.

Boar Hog sat on George's sofa. "The jack was done by a young nigga named Ali. He hangs out wit' a Chinese-looking thug named Chino. They got a house on Haygood an' Whitney. They be slingin' out of that old apartment 'round the corner on Oxford."

"Yeah, I know the spot. What the fuck is this punk—stupid?

"Naw. He just figure he ought to be runnin' shit in Studewood. Kid got a few wannabe gangster boys an' figure to take over his hood."

"The boys ready?"

"You know they is."

"Let's do it."

Ali Hunter sat on the bed in the back room of his crackhouse on Haygood Street. He was still high on adrenaline from the jack, though it had been hours since it went down. Now no one could doubt that he was the king of Studewood. The only other person who could have laid claim to that title was an old-school dude who had gotten knocked off by the HPD narcs several months ago.

What was sweet about it was that Ali Hunter had knocked off THE king, George himself, to show his peeps that Ali Hunter was the top dog in the hood. Nothing could stop him now.

He lit up a blunt as Chino walked into the room.

"It's all good, my nigga." The brother with the Oriental eyes sat across from Ali as he took the offered blunt. "We only got about fifty grand paper, but we got about three bricks."

"Hard or soft?"

"Hard."

"Good. Tell Walt to have the boys looking out in case any of them niggas from The Four-Four come looking for some get-back."

"Word. Say, that schoolteacher from Greenspoint you asked about called J-Boy a while ago. She wants to cop. I guess the glass dick is starting to get good to her."

Ali perked up. "Man, you know I want to catch that bitch before she gets too far out there. What about that nigga Mac who turned her out?"

"*J* says she coming by herself."

Ali stood and walked to the bar and reached beneath it. He handed Chino a small vial. "Here. Set it up."

Chino and the crew didn't care that Ali was into raping bitches. Hell, most of them hoes deserved it. Besides, most times Ali let him and the boys get in on the fun.

Chino left the house on Haywood and walked the block to the deserted apartments.

J-Boy met Chino on the street. "Ali glad I called you about that schoolteacher bitch?"

"Yeah. Good looking out. We got you. When she shows up, bring her up to the spot. Don't sell her nothin' yourself."

"Gotcha."

J-Boy knew that this was his big chance. He had

never been in on one of Ali's "parties," but had heard plenty of talk about them. As long as he delivered this bitch like he was supposed to, then tonight he'd be asked to join in. He worked his spot for another hour before his cell rang with her number on the caller ID.

"Hello. J-Boy, I'm turning onto Crosstimbers from the freeway. You ready for me?

" Yeah, baby. Jus' come to the same spot as before. You alone, right?"

"Yes. I don't hang with that nigger Mac no more."

"Good. See you in a minute."

Closing his phone, J-Boy ran his mind over the play he was gonna use to get her up to Ali's "fuck pad."

He recognized her black Corolla coming down Oxford Street. When the car slowed, J-Boy stepped into the street to meet it.

The woman inside didn't bother with any greeting or preamble. "Hey, I need a wholesale."

"How much?"

"Will two hundred get me a quarter?"

J-Boy was amazed at how green and new to the game this bitch was. He reached down into his shorts and pulled out a plastic bag. "You can probably do better than that. My man Chino, you know, the one you met with Mac last time, well, he's upstairs cutting up a fresh batch. Nobody's allowed up there, but since you're a good customer, and ain't gonna jack the place, I can call up and see if he will deal with you. You'll get almost twice as much shit."

The woman sat silent for a minute. J-Boy could almost see the conflict going on in her mind. This was no hulled-out crackhead (at least not yet), so she was naturally leery about going into an abandoned building with this young thug.

The thing was, though, Yvonne had been becoming more and more hooked on the rock ever since Mac had turned her on. This, plus the thought of getting maybe as much as twice the dope for her money, swayed her. She nodded her head.

While J-Boy made the call, she slipped her hand into her purse to make sure the little .22 pistol was still there. She was desperate, but she wasn't stupid. Still, she jumped when there was a tap on her passenger window. It was J-Boy, motioning for her to open the door. Shit! She hadn't even seen him move.

J-Boy got into the car, directed her to take a right at the corner of Oxford and Whitney, and to park on the street.

"Don't worry, ma. Nobody's gonna mess wit' you as long as you wit' me. You a schoolteacher, huh?"

Yvonne nodded.

"What's your name? You know mine."

"Yvonne. How long is this gonna take? I don't have a lot of time before I have to get back."

"Not long. Not long at all." J-Boy whistled in approval as she got out of the car. "Damn, ma! You a hot-looking star."

About five-seven, Yvonne was dressed in tight black slacks with a black-and-white striped blouse. With caramel skin and shoulder-length hair, average breasts, but a really nice ass and long, well-shaped legs, she was a good-looking woman.

"Thank you. Which way?"

J-Boy led her through a hole in the fence and into the complex, and Yvonne followed him up a dimly lit stairwell to the second floor. He tapped a complicated rap on the steel door in the middle of the hallway, and Chino, the light-skinned guy with the Oriental eyes, opened the door.

The room Yvonne stepped into was huge. It seemed as big as an average one-bedroom apartment..

"What's up teacher? Remember me? I'm Chino. I hear you want to cop a wholesale?"

"Hey, Chino. Yeah, me and my girls came up with two hundred. J-Boy said you could make me a deal."

"You mean there are more beautiful honeys like you out there?" He looked over at J-Boy. "Man, we got to go to Greenspoint!"

Yvonne's caramel cheeks blushed at the compliment, and her nervousness lessened. Chino was handsome and liked the way she looked.

"Say, *J*, you better get back to the block."

"Yo, Chino." J-Boy turned and left.

After the door closed, Chino pointed to the plush sofa. "Have a seat, miss teacher. As soon as I cut up our end of this cake, you can have what's left for the deuce. It should be way more than a half-*O*." He walked back to the table.

Yvonne sat and watched in fascination as Chino whacked the big, oblong block of crack into small squares. The shape of the block reminded her of the square pound cakes her mother used to make.

"Say, baby, I won't be long, but would you like a blunt and something to drink while you wait?"

Yvonne just really wanted to get her dope and get out, but she was aware that the guy was doing her a big favor with this sale. Besides, she could feel the sexual attraction between them. If she played her cards right, she might be able to turn this into a steady supply of free crack. "Sure. I like Patrón. You got any?"

Chino left the table and walked to the twelve-foot bar across the room. "I got anything you want. Look in that wooden box on the table and get the smoke."

While Yvonne's attention was diverted, he opened the vial he'd gotten from Ali and poured the contents into her glass. Then he walked over and handed her the drink. "Just relax and enjoy. I'll be able to join you in a few." He lit the blunt for her and went back over to the table.

Chino deliberately kept his back to the sofa for about ten minutes. When he thought enough time had passed, he turned to face her. Yvonne's languid pose suggested that the weed and Tequila had relaxed her. She'd undone the top two buttons of her blouse, and her push-up bra left her breasts over halfway exposed. She wasn't the best-looking woman they'd had in here, by a long shot, but something about this one made Chino horny as hell.

"I just about got your shit ready, baby. Want to come an' take a look?"

“In a minute.”

That was all the signal Chino needed. He sat next to Yvonne on the sofa, removed the glass from her hand, sat it on the coffee table, and pulled her to him. The kiss was fierce, and Yvonne responded as he knew she would. She moaned deep in her throat, and he could see her nipples harden through the thin bra and blouse.

Chino cupped her right breast, running his thumb over her nipple. Leaning forward, he lay her back on the sofa. His hands touched her everywhere. He massaged her full ass, ran his hands slowly down her tight thighs and calves, and finally squeezed her pussy through the thin, black material of her pants. Even through her clothes, he could feel the heat.

When he had her writhing, moaning, and pulling at his clothes, Chino stood and pulled her close, so she could feel his hard length between them. “Let’s go into the bedroom.”

“Okay.”

He led her to the bedroom door. “Get undressed and get in the bed. I’ve got to lock up, and I’ll be right there.”

As soon as she stumbled into the room, Chino speed-dialed Ali. “Yo, she’s ready. Come on.”

Barely a minute later, Ali slid through the front door, grille gleaming as he smiled at Chino. “I’ll call you when I’m done wit’ the bitch”

“She’s damn sure ready. Probably didn’t need the roofies. Later, my nigga. Save some for me.”

By the time the door closed behind Chino, Ali was already in the bedroom. As realization dawned in the eyes of the woman on the bed, Ali quickly stripped.

"Who the hell are you? Where's Chino?"

"Chino had to go. Besides, he lets me break in all his new hoes."

Yvonne started to sit upright on the bed. "Look, nigga. I ain't no—"

SLAP!

The open-handed blow knocked Yvonne clear across the king-sized bed.

"You whatever I say you are, bitch! An' you gon' do whatever the fuck I tell you to."

The struggle was brief, but intense.

Yvonne soon lay in the center of the bed, limp with exhaustion. Her cheeks, stomach, ass, thighs, every part of her body, ached from Ali's heavy-handed blows. She couldn't even protest as she felt a different type of touch on her skin.

"This can be as hard or as easy as you want it to be."

Ali's voice was soft, almost gentle as he rubbed his stiff dick over every inch of Yvonne. He knew from experience that the rape would be much more fun for him if she participated, especially when he knew that she didn't want to. It wouldn't be long now.

As the drug took full effect, Yvonne's thoughts became hazy and disjointed. She remembered Chino and the hot rush of desire she felt. She had lain on the bed gently touching her own wetness, imagining how good it would feel when Chino slammed his dick into her. Then images of Ali and pain flashed through her mind.

It didn't matter, though, because now something warm and heavy and hard was touching her nipples, moving up to the hollow of her throat, rubbing her cheeks, and coming to rest on her lips. She touched it with the tip of her tongue, and the combination of the sharp, salty taste and the groan that came from somewhere caused fresh wetness to flow at her center.

Eyes shut tight, Yvonne started to rotate her hips, her hands reaching for the shaft of flesh Ali was teasing her with. Pinning her hands to the bed, Ali moved so that he was positioned between her legs. He let her hands go and grasped both legs behind the knees and lifted, spreading her wide.

Without further hesitation, he slammed into her, and with only slight resistance, Yvonne's wet pussy accepted his whole length.

The orgasm hit her full strength. She screamed and rocked her body, as the spasms gripped her. Finally, satiated, her body went limp.

Ali continued to drive himself into her over and over, fucking her hard. Infuriated at her unresponsiveness, he hit her with his fist. "Move that ass, bitch!"

Yvonne's pleasure evaporated, replaced by the pain of her broken nose. She was hardly aware as Ali flipped her over, placing pillows beneath her stomach, raising her ass in the air.

When his freshly lubricated dick rammed into her asshole, Yvonne's eyes flew open. "Arghh! Stop! It hurts!"

Now Ali was in his element. For him, it wasn't about

the sex. His money and power could get him any number of beautiful, willing women. He got off on the pain and humiliation. With heavy-handed blows, he beat Yvonne about the head and shoulders as he plowed her virgin ass, her frantic movements as she tried to dislodge him only intensifying his pleasure. Gripping her hips, he fucked her harder and harder, allowing her pleas and tears to send him over the edge.

"Fuckin' whore", he groaned as he spent himself into her ass.

Yvonne lay sobbing as he reached for his phone.

"Yo, Chino. Get Drake, Bolo an' that kid J-Boy, an' come get some of this good pussy. Yeah, hurry up."

Ali flopped back onto the bed next to the sobbing Yvonne. He breathed in the smells of sex, shit, and fear. He smiled as he waited on his boys.

The big black Suburban sat idling under the shadow of a tree a block down the street from Ali's Haygood dope house. There were six men inside. Big George and Boar Hog occupied the front seats, Fred Jackson and his cousin Moochie were in the middle seat, while the Collier twins, Freddie and Frank, sat in the rear.

"What the fuck we waitin' on, *G*? Let's do this shit," Fred said.

"Chill, nigga. I know what the fuck I'm doin'." George was about to continue chewing on Fred's ass when he noticed a single headlight approaching through his rear-view mirror. "Here come the nigga we waitin' on now."

When the motorcycle coasted to a stop next to his door, George lowered the window. "What's the deal, my nigga?"

"There's three, maybe four, in the house. Was more, but two left in a hurry about twenty minutes ago. Neither was Ali, but the slim one may have been the one with the funny eyes, Chino."

"What about the lookouts?"

"Was one in the back by the fence. The other was down the street toward Yale, in some bushes."

"And?"

"They both dead." The bike rider patted the hilt of his combat knife. "You want me to go in with you?"

"Naw. We got it. Cruise around and keep watch. Hit me on my cell if there is a problem."

"Okay." The bike roared off.

Fred Jackson asked, "Who was that nigga?"

"Somebody I trust. Let's go. Just like we planned it." Big George opened his door and waited for his boys to unload and assemble.

"We're gonna do this quick. Take care of our business and get gone. Everybody in that house gets dusted. Boar, take Freddie and Frank around back. Fred, you and Moochie go through the front with me. Hit me when you in position, Bo."

The two teams split up and casually walked down the block, toward the dope house. Boar Hog and the

Colliers took to the backyard two houses away from their target.

George and his boys hesitated on the sidewalk out front, waiting for the signal. His cell phone vibrated. "Let's go!" he said, whipping his "street sweeper" from beneath his long jacket. He began to run toward the front door, Fred and Moochie right behind him.

Bolo died that day because he'd had the clap. He'd snuck off to the clinic on Yale and got treatment, and was trying to keep his condition on the low. When Chino told him in front of the boys that Ali wanted him and Drake for one of his "special" parties, Bolo, his dick still swollen and painful, had to refuse.

"What you mean, no, nigga? What the fuck is up wit' you?"

"Shit, man, I got burnt."

The room exploded with laughter.

"I told yo' dumb ass about hittin' them dopefiend hoes. Now, every time you take a piss, think about what happens when you don't listen to ol' Chino. Come on, Drake."

Drake and Chino left, and the ribbing began.

"I bet it was two o'clock in the morning and he let that nasty, used-up Maria give him a blowjob for a nickel piece." Lil' T, bubbling with laughter, could barely get out his words. "Bitch slobbed his knob so good, he jus' had to stick it."

"Fool! It wasn't that no-good—"

"Naw. Even he wouldn't stick that. It was Loose Lucy.

That ho pussy so big, the VD germs is organized into platoons." Markie reached over to high-five Lil' T.

Tyrone's deep voice interjected, "I heard them crackhead Goudeaux twins got hold of Bolo last month. Fool's dick gonna fall off, but I bet he had a good time."

"All right, muthafuckas, enough of this bullshit. Next nigga that—"

BOOM!

Following the shotgun blast, the front door blew in. There was a second explosion from the back, but Ali's men barely heard it. The sight of Big George striding into the room cradling a street sweeper, and the men fanning out behind him with assault rifles, froze them for a moment.

Bolo, standing with his hand under his shirt, was the first to die. George blew his head almost completely off. As his blood and brains blew from his head in a mist, Fred and Moochie opened up.

In seconds, all of Ali's men were down. Boar and the Collier brothers had already spread out to inspect the rest of the house. They were back in a couple of minutes with Frank holding a pillowcase and a big leather bag.

"Fred, Moochie, you know what to do." George led the way out through the back, while Fred and his cousin walked toward the back of the house.

By the time George, Boar Hog, and the two brothers had loaded themselves into the truck, flames were already rising from down the block. The Jackson cousins ran up and jumped in. George drove off.

"Neither Ali or Chino was in the house," Boar Hog said. "They're most likely at those apartments over on Oxford. Want to finish it now?"

"No. The punks will get the message. Before I'm through with them, every time they hear my name, shit's gonna run down their legs."

George slowly drove the back streets all the way back to The Four-Four.

Chapter One

Chino, J-Boy, and Drake were all fucking Yvonne at the same time. The room smelled of shit, blood, and raw sex. Yvonne's face was swollen and bloody, and nasty-looking scrapes and cuts marred her body. The men grunted, and sweat poured off them as they abused the woman.

Ali sat in a chair near the bed and watched, wondering what to do with the bitch when they were done.

A pounding on the front door whipped his head around. Who the fuck had the balls to interrupt him at a time like this, he didn't know. When he found out, though, he'd rip them a new asshole. He walked into the other room and angrily jerked open the door.

"What the fuck you want, nigga?!"

The kid at the door was too excited to be scared.

Just as it occurred to Ali that his guards must have let this boy up here for a damn good reason, the little dude started to babble. “ALI, Ali, the house on Haygood is on fire! Bolo, Lil’ T, Markie, an’ Tyrone all dead! Was Big George an’ his boys. Po-po everywhere. Everybody got in the wind. I came to tell you ‘n’ Chino.”

“What’s your name, boy?”

“J.T.”

“Well, J.T., you done good. Come see Chino tomorrow, and he’ll take care of you. Now get ghost.” Ali closed the door and slammed his fist into it. “Shit! Goddamn! That muthafucka!”

Ali was punching numbers into his cell when Chino ran into the room, butt-ass naked.

“What’s going on? What happened?”

“That nigga Big George burnt down the house and killed everyone in it.”

“Bolo?”

“Dead.”

“We’re gonna kill that big muthafucka an’ anybody with him.”

Ali closed his phone. “What we’re gonna do first is get all the money and dope we got left together and go rent a room across town somewhere. Cops are gonna be all over this place soon.”

“What about Yvonne?”

“Who?”

Chino hooked his thumb toward the bedroom.

“I’ll show you what to do with her.” Ali led Chino back into the bedroom, where Drake and J-Boy were getting dressed. Chino walked over to his pile of clothes and started to pull them on.

Ali looked down at the woman on the bed. Her shallow breathing and soft whimpers were the only signs that she was still alive. He grabbed a pillow and covered her ruined face, pressing down hard.

Yvonne was so abused and exhausted that even in her death throes, she only managed a few feeble kicks. Ali usually didn't kill the women he raped, unless it was an accident. This time, he felt it was necessary.

"Drake, you and J-Boy wrap her up in the sheets and take her out the back way. Dump her up in the woods off Greens Road. Bitch is from Greenspoint, so cops will look for some nigga in the Greenspoint Posse. When you're done, call me an' I'll tell you where we are. Let's go, Chino."

Ali and Chino left the room, leaving the other two to take out the garbage.

When Drake and J-Boy finished their grisly task, they called Ali.

"We're at the airport Doubletree Hotel, room 915."

The four men sat around the hotel room drinking cognac and smoking blunts, each was lost in their own thoughts. Things had changed for the worse. No one would admit it, but fucking with Big George was a mistake. His retaliation was only the beginning. It was war, and they didn't stand a snowball's chance in hell of winning.

Acres Home was just too big. And George King had it on lock. He had been running shit over there for more than twenty years. He was a real old-school gangster and had no problem with "planting" a nigga. The "laws" tolerated his operation because he kept it real, kept violence to a minimum, and lined their pockets.

Ali knew he had a real problem. Underneath all the bluster and bullshit, he was just like any bully and rapist, a coward when it came right down to it, so he'd sold his boys that tough-thug bullshit, which had come back to bite him in the ass. He really didn't think George would go all the way to avenge one little nickel-and-dime crackhouse in a whole different neighborhood, so now he had to do something to show his crew that he was for real.

"Chino, I want every nigga in Studewood that rides with us to strap up. We gonna continue to sling at the apartments, but we four are gonna keep a low profile. When the time is right, we're gonna teach that big muthafucka a lesson he won't forget."

"Okay, my nigga. Just tell me we're gonna do this old trick. Bolo was my boy."

"You know we're gonna make it right."

After Chino, Drake, and J-Boy left the room, Ali sat for a minute wrestling with his conscience. He had already pretty much made up his mind how he was going to handle George. His relatives in New York were a last resort. That kind of help had consequences.

He found a number in his phone and dialed. "Hello. This is Ali Hunter calling for Mr. Barnes . . . Yes, I'll hold . . . Mr. Barnes, I've got something I know you'll be interested in. It's too hot out there for me to come and see you, but if you can come here, I think it'll be worth your while. Okay . . . I'm at the Doubletree out by Intercontinental Airport, room 915 . . . Yeah, I'm alone . . . Okay, see you then."

Big George, Fred, and Moochie Jackson, and the Collier brothers all sat in Boar Hog's house on Bethune Street.

Boar Hog looked up at George from the items spread across his bed. "There's one hundred twenty-five grand, and five 'birds' (kilos) rocked up."

"Yeah. Most of it is probably my own shit. Split it all up equally 'mongst you an' the boys. Y'all let me holla at Boar for a minute. Come back an' get your shit."

All the men except Boar Hog filed out of the room. They had only gotten back from handling their business in Studewood thirty minutes earlier.

"That shit on Haygood went pretty good, but I ain't finished with them young niggas yet."

"I know. The main two weren't even there. That bitch-ass Ali and his "chink-looking" homeboy were probably at those apartments on Oxford an' Whitney."

"Don't matter. I want you to send some of the boys over there every night until they either knock them niggas or shut 'em down. Pay 'em out of my end."

"No problem."

After George left, Boar Hog split the dope and money into five piles. He thought about calling Lucille, this sister he'd been kicking it with, but decided she could wait. Him and Big George had been together for quite some time, and he owed the man, big time.

By the time the knock came on Boar Hog's back door, he'd already decided just how he was going to carry out George's instructions. It didn't take long to pay off Fred and his cousin.

Boar Hog left the Colliers till last because he wanted to talk to them alone. After describing exactly what he wanted to do, he gave each of the brothers a long look.

"You two down?"

"You know it." Freddie had that crazy grin on his face.

Frank said, "Let's go put our shit up. We'll meet you back here in a couple of hours."

When he was alone, Boar poured a big shot of Hennessy. He thought about all the shit he and Big George had done over the years. They had been through a lot. It was all part of the game to him, though. The streets had a code. You lived by it, and you died by it. What you took, you damn well had better be able to hold. And disrespecting the big dog usually got your ass bit off.

It was 4:30 a.m when the little black Toyota cruised up Haygood Street. The burned-out husk of Ali's dope house was deserted. Taking a right on Whitney, Boar Hog and the Collier brothers rode the block up to Oxford.

"Just turn and cruise down the block. When you get to the middle of the building, stop."

Frank Collier, who was driving, complied.

When the car stopped, two shadows detached themselves from the darkened entrance and headed toward the street.

Boar Hog got out from the rear, and Freddie Collier slid out the passenger door.

"Say, old school, whatcha need?"

"I need a hundred wholesale."

"Okay, no prob—"

Loud blasts ripped the night as Boar and Frank opened up on the two men who'd approached the car, and Freddie's AK swept the front of the building.

"Let's go!"

At Boar Hog's yell, Freddie dived back into the car, which sped off, leaving three men dead and two wounded. One of the dead was the kid J.T., who'd warned Ali earlier.

At Crosstimbers Street, Frank took a left, sped down to Castor, and turned right. There, they killed two more of Ali's workers at the house on Castor and Barkley.

Within the next twenty minutes, they had gone deeper into Studewood. Crossing the tracks, they hit Ali's houses on Thirty-fifth and North Main, and on Europa. After killing the three men working the Europa house, Freddie rode Thirty-third Street out to Airline and jumped on the North Loop.

Exiting the freeway at T. C. Jester, they dumped the Toyota at the park alongside the bayou. Then the three men jumped into Frank's Lexus and cruised back to The Four-Four. They had made their point.

* * *

After finishing his conversation with Chino, Ali slammed the receiver down. He paced the hotel room. Big George had wasted no time. He was taking it to Ali, no holds barred. That bitch-ass nigga had killed nine of his men and fucked up four more. Studewood was reeling. He came to an abrupt stop when he realized that George wouldn't stop until he was dead.

When the knock came, Ali jumped. He grabbed his pistol and went to the door. "Who is it?"

"Theo Barnes."

The man who walked in looked like a black mountain. He didn't have badge or gun in sight, but his very appearance screamed cop.

"Mr. Barnes, good to see you again."

"Cut the bullshit, Hunter. You don't want to see me anymore than I want to see your dope-dealing ass. The only reason you called me is, your trick ass started something you can't finish. George King is gonna plant your black ass unless I help you. The question is, why would I want to help a no-good muthafucka like you?"

"Because I can help you get something you want real bad. I'm going to show you how to take down 'the king.' "

"All right, tell me what you got. It had better be good, or you're gonna spend the rest of your short life in this room."

Chapter Two

George King sat on the edge of his bed in his palatial home on the edge of White Oak Bayou. The house sat on Bayou View Drive, a winding street that stretched from Areba Street to Garapan, and all the land along the Drive was owned by him. There were other enclaves like this either in or adjoining Acres Home, but George's was the biggest.

"What's wrong, honey?"

The big man was so involved in his thoughts that he'd never heard his wife come into the room. Dorothy King was the only thing of value that he had brought with him from Mississippi so many years ago. He raised his head and drank in the sight of her.

She was a full foot shorter than he was and weighed a hundred pounds less. Her skin was that golden color of autumn leaves. Her body was slim and well-toned, which made her breasts and behind look much larger than they were. She wore a sleeping gown and robe, and had a look of concern on her beautiful face.

"I don't know, baby, but something strange is going on."

Dorothy walked over to the bed and sat next to her husband. In spite of the fact that she had no real involvement in her man's business, she was his only real confidant. Except for their son, Chris. But he never even got to see George worried or uncertain. At least George had been insistent that Chris never become involved, though he had taught the boy everything.

"Two weeks ago, a little problem came up in Studewood, and we took care of it. There are some loose ends, but I decided to wait a month or two to collect them."

"Want the heat to die down, huh?"

That earned her a smile. "Yeah. Can't find the little nigger, anyway. Things seem to be going 'bout as usual, but I can't shake the feeling that something's up. And you know that my instincts are usually right."

"Sure I do, but there is an easy way to fix the problem."

Dorothy had long wanted George to get out of the game. They had more money than they'd ever need, not counting all their property and possessions, and she hadn't had to work as a beautician since the third month after they got here. She knew her husband was a hustler, and that he was addicted to the lifestyle, so she never pushed, resigned to the fact that George would never give up the dope game.

"I know, and for the first time, I'm beginning to believe you're right." As his wife looked at him in shock, he went on, "I'm going to talk to my lawyer an' see if I can get some of our real estate and money transferred into your name. You know I never did before, because I didn't want you held responsible for anything I was doing. Hell, most of the stuff ain't even in my name."

"The house on Lang and my car are in my name. Chris has the title to his car, too."

"Yeah, but all that was bought with a mortage and car notes. Nobody could prove they ain't legit. I want everything to be in place and legit when I step down. Chris will be in college, you can buy a beauty shop, and I'll get a garage or something. We'll get a chance to travel."

Dorothy was speechless. Her eyes filled with tears. She hadn't felt this full of love and desire for her husband since their wedding night. "Baby, you mean—"

"Yes. You finally get what you really want."

"Right now, what I really want is you."

George took her in his arms and kissed her long and hard, their tongues swirling together. When he broke it off, they were both breathing hard.

"Where is Chris?"

"Out running the streets."

"Good. This may get a little loud."

Dorothy laughed as he ripped the robe from her shoulders. Laughs turned to moans as George ran his big hands over her body. He loved the feel of her supple flesh through the silk of her gown.

"Hurry, baby," she moaned. "I'm burning up."

George had inched the hem of her gown up and now had a handful of her bare ass. His dick was rock-hard. He never stopped being amazed how such a tiny woman could have such full a full ass and tits. Lowering his head, he began to gently suck at her right nipple through her gown, his left hand tweaking the other, until they both peaked.

He picked her up and laid her in the center of the bed. As soon as his hands were off her, she pulled her gown over her head and threw it aside. George could see the glint of moisture between her legs as she opened and closed her thighs. He struggled to control his desire. It had been a long time since she had been like this, and he wanted to really rock her world.

After stripping, he lay down beside her and pulled her close. His big, thick dick bobbed against her thigh as he suckled her breasts.

Dorothy twisted and turned under him, trying to get him inside her. Her soft hands pulling on his dick made him moan deep in his throat.

George cupped her pussy, feeling the heat of her arousal. He slipped his index finger inside her, the hot juices flowing from her easing its entry, and rolled his thumb around the bud at the top of her vagina.

"Oh! Oh! Yes, baby!" Dorothy came hard, coating his fingers with her hot flow.

George continued to work her tits and pussy with his hand and mouth. When her violent movements slowed, he began to work his way down her body, nibbling at the undersides of her breasts, her abdomen, and finally, at the lips to her pussy.

Dorothy came alive again, and tried to move, but George's hands cupping her ass were just too strong. She just had to lie there and take it. He twirled his tongue from the tender skin just below her pussy, through the swollen lips, and worked it against the tiny clit at the top.

"Shit, George! You tryin' to kill me?"

He smiled. Dorothy never cursed anymore, and she always had perfect diction. He knew he had her where he wanted her now. As proof, he could feel the first contractions of her abdomen as her second orgasm approached.

He rose to his knees. Placing one hand beneath her hips, he raised her lower body so he could massage her opening with his dick. He'd always had to work himself into her before really starting to fuck, but she was having none of that now.

"Give it all to me! Now. Please, baby."

George pushed hard, his dick sliding in easily, and her pussy gripped it hard as she went over the top again. He pumped back and forth into her as she moaned and twisted under him. Her orgasm seemed to last forever. The pressure was just beginning to build up in his balls when she suddenly stopped moving.

She pushed at his chest until he backed out of her with a soft *plop*. Immediately she turned over on her stomach, her ass pointed toward him.

George was inflamed now. Grasping her hips, he rammed himself into her to the hilt. They spoke as one.

"Aahh!"

"Aahh!"

Her pussy felt like hot velvet around his dick. He pumped himself into her as hard as he could. The only sounds were the *slap-slap* of skin against skin, and the soft groans each emitted every time they came together.

"Here, baby. Here it comes!" George shot spurt after spurt into her hot sheath.

Dorothy's only answer was the tightening of her pussy around him as she came yet again.

"Damn, baby, that was the bomb."

"Go wash up, and I'll show you the bomb."

When George returned from the bathroom, Dorothy knelt between his legs and took him into her mouth. Soon she was rising and falling atop him as she rode him.

They both lost track of time and how many times they came together. It was one of those special nights that come rarely in a relationship.

Finally, they both drifted off into a deep sleep in each other's arms, so neither heard the answering machine pick up with their son's message that he would not be home that night.

Just before daybreak, George sat up suddenly. The

light that bathed the room through the closed blinds told him that something was wrong. The keypad down by the gate prevented the security lights from coming fully on when the correct entrance code was entered. Coming onto his property without entering the code would set off motion detectors and bathe the whole property in halogen light.

Recognizing that there was a breach in security, George whipped the .45 automatic from the nightstand drawer and woke Dorothy. "Get up, baby, and put something on. Somebody's out there."

"What?"

The look on her husband's face told her that the situation was serious. She did as she was told. Then she got her own gun. Glancing toward the big window as he got dressed, Dorothy said, "George?"

When George saw that she was pointing at the window, he noticed it too. The ceiling was now being bathed in a flowing montage of red and blue color.

"Shit! It's the law!"

"GEORGE KING! YOU AND ANYONE ELSE IN THE HOUSE COME OUT WITH YOUR HANDS EMPTY AND RAISED! THIS IS THE DRUG ENFORCEMENT AGENCY, AND WE HAVE A WARRANT FOR YOUR ARREST. PLEASE COMPLY WITH OUR INSTRUCTIONS AND EXIT THE FRONT DOOR UNARMED WITH YOUR HANDS IN THE AIR!"

"George! What do we do?"

He looked over at the love of his life and made his decision. It was too late to do what he had planned, but this was all a part of the risks you took when you decided to play the game.

"We do like they say, ma. Don't worry, I'll beat whatever they think they got. Just tell your story like we talked about."

After putting away their weapons, they walked down the stairs and out the front door into a nightmare—police cars from every law enforcement agency in Houston, and blinding spotlights.

"ON THE GROUND! ON THE GROUND! SHOW ME YOUR HANDS!"

Men ran up and put knees in George's back, pinning him to the ground. His arms were wrenched behind him, and his hands cuffed. For the time being, they ignored Dorothy, who was kneeling beside him,.

"Let me read him his rights." Theo Barnes stepped out of the bright glare of the lights. He bent over the prostrate George. "I know you remember. Well, I'm here to keep my promise to see you in the pen. George King, you are under arrest for the sale and distribution of crack cocaine, in violation of federal and state law. You have the right to remain silent. Anything you say can and will be used against you in a court of law. You have the right to be represented by an attorney. If you cannot afford one, the court will appoint one for you. Do you understand these rights?"

Barnes rose without waiting for an answer. "King George, I got your ass now, boy. I got me a witness. Put him in my car. Her, too, but don't cuff her. She needs somewhere to rest while we execute the search warrant."

George sat beside his wife in the rear seat of the cop's car and spoke quietly to her for almost the entire two hours it took to conduct the search. He chose his words carefully, because he was pretty sure the car was bugged. Why else would that asshole Barnes put them together?

"Do you understand, baby?"

Dorothy nodded her head.

"Don't worry, I'll call you and have my lawyer call you. This is just some personal shit between me and Barnes. It'll be okay."

Dorothy nodded again, but in her heart she knew it wouldn't be okay.

Chapter Three

Chris sat on the sofa in the house on Lang Road. It had been three weeks since the Feds had taken his father away. Three weeks of hell. Just as Big George had predicted, when the smoke cleared, all the law left them with was this house and two cars. There was money stashed away that they'd never found, but their lawyer advised them that touching it now would be tantamount to suicide.

Meanwhile, Chris watched his mom go through holy hell. He'd never realized how close his mother and father were until now. They had never shown a great deal of affection in front of him. However, with George gone, Dorothy acted like a part of her had died.

She hadn't given up, though. She had taken a job as a beautician in the shop up on the corner, explaining to Chris that, per his father's instructions, they were to live as if Big George could no longer supply them money. In effect, they had gone from millionaires to being just above the poverty level almost overnight.

As he waited for Dorothy to get home from work, Chris wished he could somehow avoid this conversation. But he and his mother were close. Really close. To not tell her what he had planned would be the same as lying to her. He didn't want to break her heart, but it was time for him to man up.

The front door opened. "Hey, baby."

"What's up, Mama? How was work?"

"It went good. You eat yet? Give me a little time, and I'll get you something."

"I'm good. I need to talk to you."

The look on Dorothy's face said she already knew and dreaded what he was going to say. "What about?"

"I know that things are gonna be hard until Daddy gets home. I can't let you carry the load all by yourself. I won't."

"Aren't you still looking for a job?"

"Every day. Things are tight out there. I even got desperate enough to apply at a couple of fast-food joints, but nothing doing."

His mother looked at him a long time. She finally sat next to him on the sofa. Looking up into his eyes, she said, "Chris, I knew your father was a hustler the day I met him. People warned me that he was nothing but trouble. There came a day when I had to decide whether to accept him as he was, and all that went with it for me, or to leave him alone. I chose to be his wife. I had no way of knowing that we would move to this city and George would go from a small-town gambler and hustler to one of the biggest dope dealers in Houston. Still, I was in it for the duration—till death and all that. I miss him so much now, but I've never regretted my choice.

"One thing he was adamant about, though, was that you never got into the game. He wanted better than that for you."

"Then why did he take me with him all those years and teach me everything? I can cook dope, shoot a gun, run game, gamble, and handle myself as well as any nigga on the street."

"He wanted you to know his world and to be able to live in it if . . . if . . . You notice that he never let you actually make a sale, or go with him to cop?"

Chris was a little taken aback to hear street language flow from his mother's lips. He realized that he'd underestimated her in more ways than one. "Yeah. He said that he didn't want my hands dirty, in case I decided to be president."

"He probably wasn't joking. Baby, I can see so much of your father in you. I know you've resented not being able to work with him. I would be lying if I said that I'm okay with what you want to do. I just want you to think it over carefully and to be really, really sure before you do anything."

"I will, Mama. You've got enough to worry about. I can take care of myself."

When he got up and left the house, Dorothy sat and

stared at a blank spot on the wall for thirty minutes. Then she got up to go fetch her Bible.

George sat in the small room reserved for attorney visits inside the Federal Detention Center.

Frank Shepherd, his lawyer, sat opposite him. He said, "George, it doesn't look good. I'll give you what they've got, and you make the decision as to how to proceed."

"What the hell do you mean, 'what they've got'? They didn't find anything on me or at my house. How can they make a case?"

"Well, George, it works a little differently with the feds. Their new conspiracy laws make it easy to get a conviction with no evidence. All they need is someone to say under oath that they knew of, or participated in a crime involving you. The trial jury is instructed to construe this as evidence against you. Half the men in federal prison on drug charges didn't get caught with any physical evidence."

"So what do you advise?"

"I think you should go to trial. You'll lose, but it'll leave an opening for an appeal, which you will probably win. Thing is, you'll do a year or two in federal prison."

"TWO YEARS!?!?!?! Bullshit!"

"The only other option is to work out a deal with the U.S. Attorney, which will mean you will serve five years."

"How much time will they give me if I lose the trial?"

"Probably five years, because it's your first offense."

"Then let's go to trial. Did you talk to Dorothy?"

"Yes. I told her again not to touch any money you may have stashed somewhere. Her and Chris have to live like you were their only source of income, and now that source was taken away."

"You look out for them, Frank . . . anything they need. You know I'm good for it, or just add it to your fee."

"George, I can help them out as a family friend, but if I start giving them large sums of money, the U.S. Attorney is gonna crawl up my ass with a microscope. I've got a family too."

"I feel you, Frank. Somehow, I think Chris will man up and take care of his mom."

Chapter Four

Fourteen Months Later . . .

Fuck! He was bleeding. He didn't think he'd been shot, but in the noise and confusion, he wasn't sure. Just like he wasn't sure if they'd come into the woods looking for him. At least they had stopped busting caps at him. Good thing, too, because his gun was empty.

That fucking Herman. He was dead, whether he knew it or not.

Big George had taught Chris early—Take disrespect from no man. So the way he saw it, there wasn't much worse disrespect than trying to shoot a brother, with no warning and no reason.

All he'd been trying to do was sling a few stones, make a few bucks, to help out the old lady. Since Big George got locked up, times were hard. These days, the only way a nineteen-year-old brother with no job and no real training could make any real money was the dope game.

Since George King, AKA Big George, had been knocked off by the feds over a year ago, things had gotten rough for Chris and his mama. The feds had frozen and confiscated their bank accounts. When they got through snatching shit, all that was left was the old house on Lang Road that they used to rent out, but lived in now, and the two cars, which were, like the house, in his mama's name. The feds had tried to take those too, but George's lawyer stopped them.

Chris had finished high school last year. An okay high-school athlete, he was a starter for the basketball and football teams, but wasn't good enough to be recruited by the colleges. And since his grades were average, there was no scholarship. And the money George had put away for college was gone too.

Chris tried, for his mama's sake, but with no real skills, he couldn't find a decent job, so he decided to help out by hustling. If dealing dope had been good enough for Big George, then it was good enough for him.

He'd been standing in The Alley this Thursday night trying to get rid of his last bag of stones. When the white Olds Ninety-Eight pulled in, he knew it was Herman and two of his boys, so he thought nothing of it. They were blasting 50 Cent, as usual. Chris just stood where he was, in the shadows at the back of The Alley.

Halfway down the drive, the car stopped. Herman killed the music and headlights, and he, BoBo, and Lee Arthur got out.

"Hey, nigga! Where you at?"

Chris didn't know what they wanted, but he was the only one back here. "Yo, what's up?"

"Whatchoo doin' in my spot, boy?"

"What the fuck you talking about? You ain't got no spot. And I got yo' 'boy' right here." Even though he knew they couldn't see, he grabbed his crotch anyway.

"I say, this my spot, and you betta get to steppin', lil' nigga."

"Fuck you! My old man was dealing here when you was still shittin' yellow."

"Fuck me? No. Fuck you!"

The sound of the gun was like an explosion, the bullet ripping a chunk of bark off the tree to Chris' right.

Chris pulled his 9 and shot back. Nervous, he missed all three dudes.

Herman, BoBo, and Lee Arthur all started shooting, and bullets whistled past him.

Fuck! I'm dead. He started to move backwards. There was a barbed wire fence at the end of the street, and behind that the woods stretched all the way to Bland. Chris misjudged the fence's position in the dark, and ran right into it. Then he felt a sharp pain in his arm. He dove through the fence and hit the ground. It felt like his thigh was on fire, but he jumped up and ran. The shooting behind him had stopped, but he ignored the trail through the woods, and struck out through the undergrowth, forcing his way east.

His car was parked in Miss Jennings's yard over on Parkes Street, on the other side of Little York, opposite The Alley. He had more bullets there. He got out of the woods, next to the dirt yard and the rows of dump trucks lined up like soldiers. Looking to his left, he could see the lights of Drew Middle School. Bleeding from the arm and thigh, Chris limped alongside the fence of the dirt yard and made his way to Little York. He still had to cross the street and go about sixty yards up to get to his ride.

Despite the pain he was in, Chris made a decision. It was time to step out from under his father's shadow. From now on the story of the King family in Acres Home would be his story.

Chapter Five

I stepped out onto the sidewalk and looked both ways up and down West Little York. To the right I could see the flashing light in front of the fire station, and beyond that, the traffic light at West Montgomery. Left, the street was clear. I watched the entrance to The Alley, but it was empty.

Hobbling across the street, I turned left. This end of Parkes Street sat almost directly across from the entrance to The Alley. There were only four houses and a church on the street, all on the right side. The left was bordered by a narrow strip of trees then the school. The end had a short path through more trees, then the rest of the street, which dead-ended at Dolly Wright. I didn't see Herman's car, but there was a police car parked at the end of The Alley, and a crowd gathered.

I limped to Miss Jennings's driveway. The front of her

house was dark. My car was pulled all the way around back. Usually, I gave her twenty or thirty dollars whenever I parked there. Bleeding, shook up, and with my gun in my hand, I decided to just leave, and pay her tomorrow. I had to get patched up and figure out a way to kill those assholes who tried to do me. What I couldn't figure out was why they'd done it.

I was really just getting started in the game. By working my ass off, I made a couple of grand a week. I didn't have the old man's connect, so I bought wholesale from this Mexican in Spring Branch and sold stones here in Acres Home. It had been my Daddy's territory, so I knew it well.

Just as I put the key into the car door, Miss Jennings's back door opened.

"Psst! Psst! Chris. Come here! Come in. Quick!" The light wasn't on, and though the voice was female, it wasn't Miss Jennings.

"Who's that?"

"It's me. Jasmine."

"Okay. Be right there."

Jasmine was Miss Jennings's niece. We were kind of friends, had known each other all our lives.

I opened the trunk, took out the box of bullets, and limped up the steps and into the house.

A hand took mine. "Come on." She led me through the dark kitchen and into a bedroom. She closed the door and fumbled around until a lamp came on.

Jas was 5-6, with skin the color of a brown paper bag. Her complexion was clear, and she had pretty hazel eyes. God, she was fine! Big, full breasts, a narrow waist, and ass for days.

"Jesus! You're bleeding!"

"Yeah. Somebody tried to cap me."

"It was that damn nigga Herman, wasn't it?"

"How did you know?"

"I'll tell you later. Sit in that chair. I'll be right back."

As she turned to go, I asked, "Where is your aunt?"

"At my house with Mama."

She left the room and came back with a big first-aid kit and some towels. That didn't surprise me, 'cause her aunt was the school nurse at Drew.

"I gotta boil some water. Take off your pants and shirt." She walked into the kitchen.

I've gotta admit, I was kinda nervous. I had always thought Jasmine was one of the prettiest girls I knew. We'd always talked and made eyes at each other, but nothing had ever come of it. We went to different schools, and I didn't live out here. Besides, when we were younger, both of us were too shy to make the first move.

Chuckling to myself, I thought, *Well, this ought to take care of the shy part.* I took off my pants and shirt and was standing there in my black boxers when she came back into the room with a bowl of hot water.

She looked me up and down. "Sit."

It was okay while she cleaned out the cut on my arm from the fence. She washed it, poured in peroxide, smeared on a cream, and wrapped it in a gauze bandage.

The trouble started when she got to the long gash on

my thigh. The wound was ugly and raw, but her hands were gentle as she cleaned it. Too gentle.

My dick started to get hard and, wouldn't you know it, the damned thing popped through the opening in my shorts.

Her eyes got big. "Damn, that's a big one. I ain't no virgin or nothing, but I only seen a couple, and they was nowhere near that big."

Naturally, my head swelled with pride.

She forgot about cleaning my wound, and reached out to touch it. That only made it harder. When she put her other hand on the crown, I jerked. "Jas."

She came around and knelt between my legs. Working the shaft with both hands, she took the crown in her mouth and bobbed her head up and down, sucking gently. It felt like heaven.

"Jas," I said again.

She raised her eyes, still sliding her mouth back and forth on me. Tightening her grip, she moved her head faster.

"I'm gonna shoot, Jas."

Jas just closed her lips tighter around my dick, so I let go, lifting my ass off the chair, and she sucked me dry.

I lay back, and barely noticed when she left.

She came back into the room, her breath smelling like toothpaste, and cleaned me off with a washcloth. Wearing a self-satisfied smile, she went back to work on my leg.

I was shocked, and trying not to show it. A lot of

brothers had shot at her and gotten turned away. She wasn't no "ice queen" or nothing, but she had a way of making you feel that having her would cost more than you were willing to pay. As much as I had liked and admired her, it never occurred to me that she might be available. Especially to me.

"Hurry up and finish that so I can take care of you."

"Don't worry about me. You're hurt. You owe me one, though. First, I got to figure out how I can take that thing."

"We'll work it out. Jas, why, I mean, what—"

"You mean, why did I do that? Look, Chris, I don't mess around much. I'm trying to find a job so I can maybe go to school." She wrapped my leg, and tied off the bandage. Then she kissed me softly on the lips. "I've been wanting to do that since I was six years old."

"Tell me about Herman."

She did.

Chapter Six

The house sat on Wilburforce Street between Sealy and Wheatly. The driveway was long and winding, ending at the carport of a small gray two-bedroom house. There were no other houses near on that side of the street, and several people kept horses on this end of Wilburforce, so a lot of the land was pasture.

The house belonged to Herman Broussard. I was here to kill him.

Directly across the street from the driveway was an old orchard. The trees bore some figs, but the apples and pears were out of season. The foliage here was thick, though.

I waited. Jasmine would be calling the house any minute now. I couldn't see it from here, but I could see the end of the drive.

Why Jas was going so far to help me, I wasn't really sure, though I was glad. Maybe it was because she felt a little guilty about Herman trying to kill me. Maybe she cared. After today's work, I would know for sure. She'd be put to the test, but it was my ass that was really on the line. I hoped she was really as down as she seemed to be.

After she had bandaged me up last night, she told me how Herman had been chasing her. She didn't like the dude. One of her friends had given him some play, and he had gotten her drunk, and him and his two boys fucked her. He kept coming by Jasmine's house and giving her shit. Yesterday, afternoon, when she was on her way to Miss Jennings's house, he stopped her. She'd told him that when she left her aunt's house, she was coming over to The Alley to look for me.

I crouched down quickly among the fruit trees as headlights shone onto the road from the driveway. It was Herman's Ninety-Eight. He was on his way to pick up Jasmine. As soon as the taillights disappeared up Sealy, I crept out of the trees. I was in a hurry because I needed to be inside the house when they got back. I knew it would be just him and Jas because she told him that she'd heard what happened to her friend.

At the carport I pulled on my gloves. The backyard was fenced in, and I knew that he kept a pit bull. When I rattled the fence, the dog rushed around the house. I shot it three times. Then I jumped over and poked the dog with my foot, to make sure it was dead, before dragging it under the house.

Kicking at the back door didn't do any good. It held solid. I busted out the glass in the kitchen window and climbed in. There was a huge bar set in brackets across the door. I walked through into the front room. There was a closet in the wall near the door. I stepped into it, pulled the door almost all the way closed, and waited, my hand sweaty around the grip of my pistol.

It wasn't long before I heard the car coming. Then the headlights went out, and I could hear voices outside the door.

"Stop. Wait until I'm ready." It was Jasmine's voice.

"I can't wait, baby," came Herman's gruff response. "I been waiting a long time. I gots to have me some of this."

Her laugh sounded forced. "At least wait until we get inside. I ain't one of your crackhead hoochie mamas."

Keys jangled at the door. Then I heard it open and close.

"Stop. Damn. You don't have to be so rough."

"You little bitch, you ain't seen rough. That ass is mines now. Think you too good for me? Well, if you is real good, maybe I won't call my boys, like I tol' 'em I would, an' let them have a taste. Like we done yo' bitch friend, Linda."

I stepped out of the closet. "Maybe if you real good, I won't blow your little dick off and let my boys use you for pussy." I don't know why I was so mad. My hands were shaking with anger. Shit, I wasn't this pissed when the assholes shot at me.

As Herman whirled at the sound of my voice, Jasmine stepped away from him. His hand whipped behind his back.

"Please try it. I'll cap yo' ho ass."

He brought both hands up, palms out, anger and fear mingled on his face.

"Jas, get the gun out of his belt."

She pulled the automatic from behind him and cracked him hard on the head with the barrel—"Bitch-ass nigga . . . treat me like that"—then ran over to stand by me.

As Herman grabbed his head, I looked at her and grinned. She definitely had spirit. I motioned toward the sofa. "Sit down."

He went to the couch and sat.

"Take off all your clothes."

"What?"

"I said, 'Get naked,' nigga. Don't make me have to say it again."

Jasmine giggled. "His lil' ol' dick ain't half as big as yours."

I could see the anger and shame mount in his face. Another minute and he would do something stupid. I needed something from him before I finished it.

"Hush, baby," I said to Jas. "Where is your dope and your money? You and your flunkies tried to cap me last night. You owe me. I take your shit an' we even . . . long as you don't fuck with my girl no more."

"Fuck you, nig—"

I shot him in the right leg, and Jas jumped. I had missed the kneecap and hit the shinbone.

Herman screamed as blood shot from the wound.

"Next one's in your dick—Where?"

"Behind the dresser. Shit! You shot me! Behind the dresser!"

I took his pistol from Jas and gave her mine. "If he moves at all, just point it and pull the trigger. Keep pulling it."

"I know how to shoot. I hope he moves. Killing this ho would be fun."

I ran to the big bedroom. The dude was sloppy. Clothes were everywhere. A big old-fashioned dresser with a mirror was standing against one wall. With effort, I slid it out. In a hole cut into the sheetrock was a metal box about two feet square.

I yanked it out and set it down on the dresser. I flipped the catches and opened it. Two kilos of powder and a bread bag with ounce cookies were inside. I could see some green bundles of cash beneath the coke. I closed the box and turned to go.

On a hunch, I flipped up the mattress. Nothing. When I lifted the box springs, there was a covered shoebox wedged under the wire. Working it out, I took off the lid. It was full of cash.

When I went back up front, Jasmine was holding Herman at gunpoint. Rocking back and forth in pain, blood continued to pour out around his fingers.

I handed the shoebox to Jasmine and took the gun. Without hesitation, I shot Herman three times, twice in the chest, and once in the head. Blood and bits of flesh flew, and the stink of gunpowder filled the room.

Jasmine's face paled, but she didn't say anything.

I placed the metal box on the floor and put both guns in my belt. "Let's go. Did you touch anything in here?"

She shook her head.

I picked up the box, and we walked toward the door. Since Herman's house was isolated, I didn't think anybody would have heard the shots. If they did, they probably wouldn't have called the law anyway. The fields and pastures around it were used for target practice by lots of people. I had even tried out my gun there when I bought it.

At the door I said, "Wait."

Pushing Jas out onto the porch, I set the box down again and went back in. I needed his cell phone. I found it in his pants, took it and put it in my pocket. I returned to Jas, got the dope box, and we walked away.

We waited at the last curve in the drive until there were no car lights in either direction. Then I hustled her across the street and into the orchard. On the other side of the orchard was an old, abandoned house, where my Lexus, or rather my old man's, was parked.

I threw the boxes in the trunk, and we got in. I looked over at Jasmine. Her face was flushed, and she looked scared. "You did good. Real good. We make a good team. And we got paid. Can you get away from home for a couple of days?"

"Why?"

"Because we ain't through yet. When we're done, I

want you to come to my mama's with me. We'll chill for a minute. I'll be good."

She had to smile at that. "I guess so. What else do we have to do?"

I pulled out Herman's cell phone. "Here's the deal."

Chapter Seven

Our next stop was Bethune Street. An old-school crackhead named Boar Hog lived there. I didn't know him too well, but I heard that before he got on the pipe, he was a bad-ass dude. My old man trusted him, so I figured I could too. My work today wouldn't be finished until I took care of Herman's two road dogs.

I pulled up in front of the little yellow house where Boar Hog lived, and hit my horn. I didn't want to be here too long, because the whole street was a sales yard for crack. It would have been a disaster if the law came down here and searched me now.

A crackhead sister named Lucille stuck her head out the door.

"Where is Boar Hog?" I shouted.

"He in the back."

"Tell him to put that thing down and come talk. It's Big

George's son, Chris." I got out of the car and sat on the hood.

Boar Hog came around from behind the house. A big, stocky man, he looked tough enough to wrestle a grizzly bear. His beard was unkempt, and his clothes were wrinkled and dirty. The first two fingers on his left hand were missing at the knuckle.

"What's up, youngster? How your old man? You been to see him lately?"

"He's all right. I talked to him the other night. I'm going down there next week."

"What you need?"

"Say, man, you don't really know me, so I'll be straight up. My daddy says you're good people. He said if I ever needed help, come to you. I've got a problem. Three dudes tried to cap me last night. Two of them are still running around. I need to take care of it."

"What about the third?"

I just looked at him.

"Oh. When you gonna take care of business?"

"Tonight. In just a little bit. I can get them both to come to the back of The Alley. They'll both be strapped, and I want to do it quick and get gone."

"Who?"

"BoBo and Lee Arthur."

"Herman's boys. I don't like them little punks anyway. They go for bad. Where's Herman?"

"Gone."

"Let's do it."

"Just like that? You don't want to know what's in it for you?"

"If you yo' old man's son, I'll be all right."

"Get in. This is my girl Jas. You know Boar Hog."

They both spoke.

"Okay, we're gonna park at Miss Jennings' house. You go down Cathcart and come through Byron's backyard and over the fence. I'll come from the dirt yard. Jas will get Miss Betty out of her house. Them two niggas will come to the end thinking they're waiting for Herman. When they get out of the car, we do 'em. You go back up Cathcart and come out by the hamburger stand. Go through the schoolyard to Miss Jennings. I'll come up Parkes and meet you behind the house."

"I need a piece. I sold mines."

I handed him Herman's gun. Turning to Jas, I said, "Your aunt already at your house?"

She nodded.

The Alley was Section 8 housing. The short street held twelve little clapboard houses crowded in together, each one housing about eight poverty-stricken people. Convenient to Little York, it was a spot where several different people sold crack. There was only one way in for a car. It was perfect for an ambush, too.

"Okay, baby, make the call."

The first number programmed into the phone must have been Herman's mother, because I heard Jas say, "Sorry, ma'am. Wrong number."

The next one was it.

"Hello. Lee Arthur, this is Jasmine. Herman says for you and BoBo to meet us in The Alley in thirty minutes. He rented Miss Betty's house in the back . . . Oh, he in the bathroom. He can't handle this pussy. He say he need some help. He told me to tell you if we ain't there when you get there, wait. And something about 'remember last time.' Okay, I got to go. Bye." She hung up.

I could just see those two shitheads drooling at the thought of getting between Jasmine's thighs.

"Good girl. Now go get Miss Betty out of there."

We took the stuff out of the trunk at her aunt's house. I set it on the kitchen table, gave Jas a wad of money, and sent her on her way.

"When we going over there?"

"As soon as Jas pulls out with Miss Betty. There she goes now. You ready?"

"Let's go."

We walked together down Parkes. Boar Hog took a right toward Cathcart, and I went left, toward the dirt yard. By the time I came to The Alley, just behind the end house, I knew we only had a few minutes to wait. I put in a fresh clip, and chambered a round.

Headlights swept into The Alley. I really didn't have to look to know it was Lee Arthur's Impala. 50 Cent told me. He was still blowing about the "Candy Shop" when the shooting started.

Lee Arthur flung backwards as the bullets hit him, and BoBo lay in front of the car, directly in the headlights, half his head gone.

I faded back into the woods, along the dirt yard fence, and back up to Little York.

I was just opening Miss Jennings's back door when Boar Hog showed up. We went inside.

"Piece of cake," he said, like we'd just gone and picked up a pizza.

I went to the metal box on the table and took out five thousand dollars and two cookies of crack. I put them in Boar Hog's hands. "I appreciate what you did, man. Jasmine will be back in a few minutes, and I'll give you a ride home. You can keep the piece. We straight?"

"Damn right, youngster. You sho are yo' daddy's son. Anytime I helped him, he always took care of me."

"Say, Boar Hog, I'm going to see my daddy soon. When I come back, I'm really going to work. No more of this small hustling. I'm going to stack some paper. You need a job?"

"Sure do."

"Can you back off the pipe? It fucks up your business. You know that. We can really get paid, man."

"I'm-a try. It's hard, though. That damn rock calls to you like sweet pussy. Come see me when you ready to crank it up. I'm-a break. Don't need no ride. It's right up the street. All the laws over at The Alley anyway. Later."

"Yo, later, bro."

When I heard Jasmine pull in, I had just finished going through both boxes. I had two birds of powder, eighteen ounces of crack, and sixty-five thousand dollars cash. For me, that was a hell of a lick. Now I really needed to see my old man. It was time to go to the next level.

Jasmine burst through the back door. Her eyes lit up when she saw me. "You made it! Cops are all over The Alley. I let Miss Betty out, but I couldn't see what was going on. Where's Boar Hog?"

"He went home."

We stood there looking at each other a moment. Then she ran into my arms. She felt good there.

I really wanted to fuck her, but then again I didn't. I fucked around with a lot of different girls, and it didn't mean nothing to me. From what I could see, beyond getting your rocks off, women were nothing but trouble. The next nigger wouldn't have no more trouble than I did getting them to drop their panties.

As long as a brother was on top, had paper, a ride, and sharp clothes, they were all up under you. Let things go bad, though, and they were with the next nigga with the bling. These young broads were nothing like my mama and her generation. I wasn't the one. No way was I gonna get caught up like that.

In just the little time since last night, though, I could see that Jas might be the exception. I could talk to her. She was all the way down for a nigga. Shit, truth was, I trusted her. The only other woman I could say that about was Mama. These thoughts made me all the more sure that when I fucked her, things would change. I wasn't gonna push for that. I liked just the way things were with her. There were plenty others I could fuck.

I told her, "We'll go by and give your aunt and your

mama some money. Then we'll go to my house. I got some stuff I want to talk to you about. Tomorrow, we'll burn up Memorial City Mall. Maybe buy you a car."

"Hold on, baby. Let's just do the mall. The car can wait."

See what I mean? Most girls gonna get all they can from a brother when they up. When he's down, they don't know him.

"We'll talk about it. Way I see it, half that shit is yours anyway."

"You keep my half. Invest it for me."

I didn't know where she was going with this, but I got the strong feeling that I had better watch my ass with this one. All of a sudden I was anxious to let Mama give her the once-over. Mama's bullshit detector was without par.

We left.

Chapter Eight

Herman, BoBo, and Lee Arthur were dead. Maybe a part of me felt bad about that, but it wasn't a very big part. That was the game. For whatever reason, Herman had decided to eliminate me. Whether it was over the dope, or because of Jas, it didn't make much difference. I got him first. Perhaps he'd done me a favor, though.

I started slinging stones out of financial necessity. When Big George got knocked and things went bad for me and Mama, I had to find a way to help out. Since I was raised around the dope game, it was only natural that I turn to it. I wasn't motivated by trying to make as much money as I could, or fancy cars, clothes, or jewelry. Not then. I just wanted to make it.

Running through the woods bleeding, bullets flying all around me, it kind of changed my attitude. A close call with death can be a real reality check. Every time I hit those streets, my life or my freedom was at risk. It didn't make sense to play the game if I wasn't playing to win, which in the dope game meant having more money, more dope, and more power than anyone else, and being willing to do whatever it takes to get it.

I had also discovered something about myself. I never knew I could kill. If the motivation was there, I could shoot another person with no hesitation. To me, my daddy was the gentlest man I knew. From all the stories I'd heard, though, he was the same way. He did whatever it took.

I figured my mistake was trying to do two things that were totally opposite. On one hand, I was trying to hustle cash for me and Mama. On the other, I was trying to honor Big George's wish for me not to be like him. It was bound to get me fucked off sooner or later if I didn't decide who I was. Now, I had made my decision. And I knew more people were going to die by my hand.

All this went through my head as Jasmine and I drove to Mama's house. We lived on Lang Road, between West 43rd and Hempstead Highway, just north of Spring Branch. As I pulled in behind Mama's Acura, I decided I needed a more nondescript ride than the Lexus. I also needed to put a crew together.

When I let us into the house, Mama was behind the ironing board as she watched television. She was small, light-skinned, dark-eyed beauty from Natchez, Mississippi, where her and Big George grew up.

"What's up, baby?

"Mama, this is Jasmine Hughes. Jas, my mama, Mrs. Dorothy King."

"Nice to meet you, Mrs. King."

"You too, baby."

"Mama, I asked Jasmine to stay with us for a couple of days."

Having spent my whole life trying to read Mama's moods, I immediately saw what was on her mind, if not her face. While she'd been here worried sick that I would end up like my daddy, or worse, I had been somewhere shacked up with this little whore. To make matters worse, I had the nerve to bring her here to her house.

Before she could open her mouth, though, I opted for the pre-emptive strike. "Mama, Jasmine is my friend. We've never had sex, but she did save my life. There's a little trouble, but it will blow over. She needs to hang out in the spare room for a couple of days. Helping me may have put her on the spot. I need a shower." I took Jas' elbow and led her to the sofa. "Sit down, baby."

It was pure joy to watch Mama's reaction. I had nuked her good. She knew I wouldn't lie to her, and in one breath I had addressed all her concerns and elevated Jas to sainthood. Now she was on her own. I chuckled all the way to my room.

When I had showered and put on a sweat suit, I walked back into the living room. Mama and Jas were laughing and talking like old friends. The way they stopped when I walked in made me feel like the butt of a joke, but I knew better than to ask.

"Boy, go bring this girl's stuff in so she can get comfortable. Where are your manners?" Mama looked at me with an expression that said that I'd done something right for a change.

I did what she said. I put the box with the money and the metal case with the dope in my room, and Jasmine's overnight bag in the spare room.

Mama insisted on fixing us something to eat. I knew Jas had won her over when she made Jas serve me instead of doing it herself. Now I had to watch out for both of them.

I got up the next morning, and Mama had already left for her job as a beautician at Marie's Beauty Salon up on the corner. Since I was now paying the bills, she was saving to buy her own chair, which would increase her earnings by thirty percent.

I stood in the kitchen doorway and watched Jas cook breakfast, my dick hard as a brick. She had on a nightgown, and that body was bangin'!

Feeling my eyes on her, she looked over her shoulder. "Hey, breakfast will be ready in a minute." She turned back to the stove.

I walked over and stood close behind her.

Feeling my hardness against her ass, she leaned back into me. "The food's gonna get messed up if you keep that up."

I reached out and turned her around. She looked up at me, and I had to kiss her. Her big tits were soft against my chest, and she felt good in my arms.

"Now is not the time for this. We need to talk."

That sounded good, but I was horny as hell. I needed some pussy. I made up my mind what to do about it and stepped back.

"I'm gonna wash up and get dressed. We got to talk, then we got a lot to do."

She looked both relieved and disappointed.

I went to get dressed, and she finished breakfast.

When we sat down to eat, I told her, "Jas, I've been thinking. I want to blow up. I'm gonna be the crack king of The Four-Four. You going to help me?"

"You know what you talking about? A lot of niggas ain't gonna like that. It's going to be hard. You could get hurt. Me, too."

"That's just it. I damn near got killed the other night, and you almost got gang raped at the very least, and we hadn't done nothing to nobody. Fuck that. If we got to take them kind of chances, at least let's get paid. I got a plan. And I'm gonna have help. You with me?"

"Wasn't I down with you last night? I grew up out there. I know everybody."

"I know that, but I don't want you for the street shit. I need somebody I can trust. To have my back. To hold my money. If we do it right, in a couple of years, we can have it all."

"We? Is this going to be just business, or are you talking about something more?"

I took a deep breath and opted for the truth. "I want you so bad, it hurts. What I really want is to have you both ways. I really need you on the business tip, but if we are together as man and woman, I'm scared it might fuck us up."

She looked at me a long time. "I'm in on the business end. I'll keep my own money. I got your back. When you ain't scared no more, come talk to me."

I couldn't read her eyes. She got up to go get dressed. She didn't sound mad, and she agreed to be down, but I still had the feeling that I had fucked up.

I pulled out my cell phone, called Marie's, and asked for Miss Marie. When she came on, I asked if she could come to the house for a minute without saying anything to Mama. She sounded suspicious, but I told her it was important.

Fifteen minutes later there was a knock on the door.

Marie LeBlanc was a Creole from New Orleans. She was near forty, Mama's age, and she was beautiful. When she came in and saw Jas, she relaxed. She probably thought I had called her over to hit on her. Not that it was a bad idea, but I wanted to do business.

I smiled. "Miss Marie, I know you're busy, so I'll come to the point. How much will it cost Mama to buy her own chair?"

"Five thousand. After she pay me that, she only pay me two hundred a month. Everything else is hers, yes."

"Wait a minute, please."

I went into my room and got five grand. I put the stack of bills into her hand. "She doesn't know about this yet. You can tell her later today. Say it was from me and Jasmine."

She started to count. "She already give me two thousand. Ever' week she give me somethin'. Here."

"No. Give it to Mama. Tell her I'll see her when she gets home."

"You a good son, Chris."

This time when she looked at me, her eyes were more appraising. Maybe it's a good thing Jas was there. Like I said, she was a beautiful woman.

I had Jas fill out some forms. Then I gave her twenty thousand dollars. "I'm taking fifteen, and leaving the other twenty-five for business. We've got some shopping to do."

Chapter Nine

Jasmine and I spent the rest of the morning at the Memorial City Mall. She had good taste in clothes. I wished I had taken her to The Galleria, or Clear Lake Mall, so she could have gotten some exclusive shit. She seemed happy, though. Good. I wanted her and Mama situated so that when the shit hit the fan, and the blood started to flow, none of it would get on them.

Before any of that happened, I needed to talk to Big George. I needed his advice and his connections. I had sent a visitation form for Jasmine this morning. Since she would be handling the behind-the-scenes shit, I wanted her to be able to ask him for advice too. By tomorrow, she should be on his visiting list. I was going to take just her with me to see him. Mama didn't need to hear this.

I let Jas put together a couple of fly outfits for me. I

even let her get me fitted for a white tux. That was my peace offering.

On the way home, we stopped at a used car lot on Hempstead, and I bought a three-year-old Dodge truck for eight thousand cash. The Benz and Bentley could come later. I planned to let Jas drive Mama's Acura, and leave the Lexus at home. When we got back to the house, I told Jas to chill for a while till I got back. I was going to start putting my crew together.

My first order of business was to get my dick wet. It was a little after one p.m., when I headed for Linda's crib.

Linda Olivares was a stripper at a club on Highway 290. I'd met her there the year before. We got together now and then to fuck. It never went any deeper than that, but for both of us, it was enough. I was hoping she was still home, and alone. Jas had me hotter than a two-dollar pistol.

Linda opened her door, wearing nothing but a thong. "Chris. Come in. I'm just getting ready for work. What's up?"

I pushed past her, already unbuttoning my shirt. I dropped my pants and shorts and stepped out of them.

She looked down. "Oh, it's like that, huh?" She gave a little laugh. "I don't have much time, but we can't have you running around like that. You might scare the school children."

I grabbed her and kissed her, running my hands over her lush body. She was a couple of years older than me, brown-skinned and slim. Her breasts were huge, and real, her ass nice and round. Except for her butt being smaller, she kind of reminded me of Jas, the way she was built.

"I'm sorry I couldn't call. When I'm like this, it's gotta be you. You take it all without squirming."

She groaned and moved her ass back and forth, my stiff dick trapped between her legs. When I bent and took her nipple in my mouth, she moaned. "Aaah."

I reached down to her waist and ripped the thong apart. I turned her around and bent her over the arm of the sofa, spread her ass cheeks, and prodded with my dick until it slid in. Her pussy, as always, was hot and wet.

"Oh." She gasped as I slid all the way in.

Holding her by the waist, I began to fuck her. Soon the only sounds were our passionate moans, and the slap of our flesh coming together. I could feel her juices flowing around me as she pushed back to meet my strokes.

"Give it to me, baby. I'm ready." I fucked her harder.

Her ass cheeks flexed as her orgasm hit her, and I was right with her, flooding her box with my seed. After twisting together for a few moments, I pulled her upright. I pressed her back close to me as I slipped out of her.

"I needed that, baby. You're the best."

"Boy, you were just horny. If you came to see me more often, that wouldn't happen."

"I've been busy. I'm busy right now. I just had to come get some relief. I need one more favor."

"What?"

"Take this couple hundred dollars and buy you some new thongs. Maybe some of those panties with a built-in hole, so I don't have to wait."

She laughed again. "Boy, you a fool. Go wash off and get out of here. I got to go to work. For real, though, come see me when you got more time. We need to party."

"Bet."

I went to clean up, and in a few minutes was back in my truck. I dialed a number on my cell as I drove away.

"UTMB. May I help you?"

"Yes. I'd like to speak to Victor King in receiving, please."

"May I ask, who's calling?"

"His cousin, Chris."

This was the usual routine with the Medical Center receptionist. A few moments on hold, and I heard a familiar voice,

"*Dick-on*! What's up?"

"Yo, Slick. Same old shit. What you doing this evening?"

"Nothing much. What you need?"

"I need to see you at Mama's tonight. It's important."

"Anything wrong?"

"Naw. Just business."

"I'll be there. Tell Aunt Dot to cook the whole cow. Later." He hung up.

Vic was my first cousin. We were the same age and had grown up together. I mean, shared the same crib. My middle name was Dichon, and he called me *Dick-*

on. He was the only person I let kid me about the size of my rod. He came to Houston with his mom, Big George's sister, after her divorce, and they lived in South Park, across town. He was family, and I trusted him with my life. That was about to be put to the test.

I drove over to Acres Home. My first stop was Boar Hog's place. I parked the truck, walked around the house, and knocked on the back door.

I heard a female voice say, "Who is it?"

"Chris."

"Chris who?"

I walked in. The same girl I had seen before was walking into the kitchen from the other direction.

"What you doin' walkin' in here like that?"

"Chill, Lucille. Where he at?"

"Say, Lil' King," Boar Hog said, "come on back."

He was sitting in an easy chair in the front room, with a forty-ounce OE (Olde English) in his hand, but no pipe. His eyes looked clear, maybe a little red. I was surprised to see that he obviously wasn't high on crack.

"You on the wagon?"

"Kinda. I took me a wake-up this morning, and thought about what you said. I been slingin' the rest. Doin' pretty good too."

"Good deal. Let's take a ride."

Boar Hog reached under the seat cushion and pulled out a bag of rocks. "Lucille!"

She came in from the other room, straight shooter (crack pipe) in her hand, the tip still smoking. The blast had her eyes slightly glazed as she looked at Boar Hog.

Even though the dope had poached the flesh off her frame, I could see that with a few pounds on her, she would be a nice-looking woman. What a waste.

Boar Hog counted out ten stones. “That’s ten twenties. When I get back, I want one fifty, or my dope. And it better be the same size. Understan’ me, ho?”

“Yeah, Bo, I got it.” She walked off clutching the dope like gold.

Boar Hog followed me out to the truck. As we turned around in the driveway, I said, “What you wanna bet, when we get back, your money’s short?”

“No bet, youngsta. I already knew I was gonna have to slap her ass around when I gave it to her. She knew it too. But she all right. She’ll have most of it. I’ll lean on her an’ make her get the rest out of what she has to smoke. Or she’ll hustle it with a couple of blowjobs.”

I shook my head. Dope fiends had their own set of rules. “Say, I told you last night I was gonna come up. I’m putting a crew together—me, Jas, my cousin Vic. I want you too. You ready for this?”

“I told you I was.”

“Listen, man, no disrespect, but I don’t fuck around about my paper.”

“Listen, son, I know your old man. He trusted me. I worked for him, and he never came up short. Shit, we did make that thing last night look like a picnic. Me and them hoes at my house, we do all right. We can stay high an’ keep the lights on. I’m only doin’ this ’cause you Big George’s son. Jus’ like las’ night. He looked out for me. When I say I’m witcha, I’m witcha.”

I felt where he was coming from. I remembered my old man telling me to never underestimate a man because of the situation he found himself in. Just like a few minutes ago, I had seen that Lucille, without the pipe ravaging her, could have been a fine woman, I could see that the dude I was sitting next to was a whole different man than when he was on crack.

"Sorry, man. I feel ya. You in. Cool?"

"No sweat, youngsta. When we get down?"

"I'm going to see my old man tomorrow. We start after I get back."

"Okay. Let me out here at the sto'. Give that bitch time to fuck up a little."

I drove to Miss Jennings's house. She was sitting on the front porch with Uncle Lloyd, the old man from next door. Everybody figured they were sweet on each other, but there was no proof, but I thought they were too old to do the nasty.

"Hey, baby. Where my niece?"

"How y'all doing? She wit' my momma. We'll be back out here Sunday or Monday. I just stopped by to see how you were doin'."

"I'm fine, son. That your truck?"

"Yes, ma'am."

"It's pretty. You kinda sweet on Jasmine, ain't you?"

"Now, Clara," Uncle Lloyd said. "Leave the boy alone. Stevie Wonder could see what's goin on. Now you treat her right, hear?"

"Yes, sir. Me and Jas are real good friends. I am gonna take care of her."

"Friends, right. Y'all just better not be making no babies. That girl need to go to college. You tell your momma I said hello. Tell her to come see me some time."

I waved and took off.

When I made it back to Mama's house, Vic came out to meet me. We hugged.

"What's up, cuz? Who's the fine-ass star in there? Man, a world-class ass! Hook me up."

I looked upside his head, real crazy-like.

He busted out laughing. "Got you. I know that's yo' girl. Damn, she is bad, though. Besides, I ain't following that horse dick of yours. Might fall in. Remember Natalie?"

I bristled. I sure did remember Natalie, and how she took on our whole little clique back in Mississippi one night when we were all drunk and high on that chronic. I punched his shoulder. Hard. "Enough of that shit, Red. Watch how you talk about mine."

Vic whistled. "I'll be damned. You got it. Bad. I don't believe it."

"Don't be crazy. I never ain't never touched her. Not really. She's my friend, and our partner. Just don't fuck with her."

"Partner, what's up?"

"You know I been slinging a little since Daddy got knocked?"

"Yeah? And?"

"Well, last night some shit went down. I had to drop some dudes. Dodging them bullets made me realize that if I'm goin' to hustle, then I ought to do it right. And big. I'm putting together a crew. We're gonna come up out in The Four-Four."

"Uncle George know?"

"I'm going to see him tomorrow. I want you with me. I got to have people I can trust, who got my back. It'll be me, you, Jas, and Boar Hog, this old-school friend of Daddy's."

"You know I'm with you. I was ready to quit that bullshit job anyway. It don't pay nothing."

"Call me Sunday morning. We'll all get together. Let's go in and eat."

Chapter Ten

By 7:00 the next morning, Jas and I were on our way to Beaumont, Texas, eighty miles from Houston. That's where my Daddy was. He had called last night to let me know he'd added Jasmine to his visitation list, as I'd asked. He also wanted to know who she was.

"One day she may be your daughter," I told him.

I think Jas may have heard, 'cause she was looking at me real funny when I gave the phone to Mama.

Jas was quiet until we got to Interstate 10, a few miles from the house. "I appreciate you letting Aunt Clara know that I was all right."

"No problem."

"Look, I told you I'd be your partner. I do what I say. You set it up, and tell me what you need me to do. If you need somebody set up like the other night, cool. If you need me to bust on a nigga, cool. We do it your way first. I'm okay with that."

I shut up and drove. I didn't quite know where she was headed with this, but I knew there was a trap in there somewhere. When the time was right, I would lay down the law. I cut a look at her. Damn. The law wasn't the only thing I would lay down soon. We jammed Majic 102, listening to the heavy rap beat all the way to the federal prison complex.

Surrounded by chainlink fences, the medium and low-security institutions looked like college campuses, except for the razor wire and shotgun-packing perimeter trucks. (Daddy was at the low.) And the camp didn't have a fence at all.

We signed in and waited about thirty or forty minutes before he walked through a rear door into the room.

George King was a big man. He looked like a weightlifter. His short hair was starting to go gray at the sides.

His handsome face split into a grin. "What's up, sonny?"

"Hey, Daddy. This here is Jasmine."

"So I heard. Hello, pretty lady."

Jas smiled and blushed. "Hi, Mr. King. Pleased to meet you."

They shook, and we sat down.

The room was about half full. We chose seats toward the back, away from the security desk. If we talked low, the inmates and visitors nearest us couldn't hear.

"I wired you five hundred dollars yesterday. Is that

enough? I didn't want to send enough that they would start to wonder."

"I appreciate it, son. It was more than enough. Your momma looks out. She tells me you take care of the bills. I'm proud of you."

"I hope you are still proud of me when I leave here. I need to tell you some things. Don't get mad now." Now that the moment was upon me, I was anxious. No way was he gonna like what I had to say.

"Just tell it."

I told him all of it, from the small-time hustling to Herman and his boys. The way I felt about it all. I didn't hold back. There was no man in the world whose opinion mattered more to me than his.

Big George went still. He looked into my eyes for what seemed like a long, long time. Then he blew out his breath. "I had hoped you would never have to get into this game. I wanted more than that for you. I wasn't smart, though. The feds took almost all of my shit. They never caught me doing anything, but I didn't know the law. Some snitch said he bought dope from me over a period of time. He got his friend to back up what he said. I got convicted of conspiracy, and they gave me ten years.

"I'll be honest with you, son. Really, I wish you wouldn't do this, but if you are, then you need to do it right. One thing you got dead right. If you are gonna be out there, then you might as well get paid. Dead for a twenty-dollar rock is the same as dead for a hundred birds."

"I already got a crew, Daddy."

"Who?"

"Jas, here, Vic, and Boar Hog."

"Would you let any of them hold all your money, or all your dope?"

"Yeah."

"Could you let Vic or Bo spend the night in the house with Jasmine without worrying about them trying to knock her off? She's mighty fine."

Jasmine started to bristle.

I put my hand on her arm, thinking about what he'd just said. "I trust them, and I damn sure trust her."

"Then you got your crew. First thing you need to do is get Jas a place somewhere out of the hood, where you can live and keep your money. Make sure the place is in her name, and that nobody knows where it is, except for your crew.

"She can work in the hood. You need to get her a small business or something. Don't get carried away, and don't make it a nightclub. You can be her best customer. All you got to do is give her money, and let it seem like it was made through the business. That way, you pay taxes on it, and it becomes legit. Now she can build up a bank account. When you buy shit, she can show where the money came from, and they can't take it. Most of the guys in here are white collar. They got knocked for stealing shitloads of money, and they know how to flip it and hide it. I wish I had known this shit before. Jas don't ever touch no dope, or hang around your business deals. That's why they couldn't mess with your momma. Got it?"

"Yeah."

"I guess you know that when you start moving real weight out there in Acres Home, it's gonna get real ugly real quick, huh?"

"I know, Daddy."

Big George looked at me. "Yeah, I guess you do. You a man now, and I got to let you make your own way. One thing, them coupla birds you got ain't gonna hack it. I can help with that." He got up and walked to the desk in the middle of the room, where the female guard sat behind a console of equipment. He said something to her, and she smiled.

George picked up the pen and paper she laid on the counter, sat back down, and wrote quickly. "Here's a phone number and a name. It's my connect. Wait three days, until Wednesday afternoon, then call him. Tell him who you are, then do what he says. The first time won't cost you nothin'. It's what he owes me. After that, you pay as you go."

I knew what he was doing was cashing in his insurance policy. For me. This thing with his connect was what he'd planned to use to come up when he got out. He was trusting his future plans to me.

"You know what really put me on top? The quality of my shit. This dude will show you how to cook all the "cut" out of the powder. You'll lose weight, but it'll be kick-ass. They all got two types of dope they sell. You'll be getting the good shit to start with. Sell your weight a little smaller, and they'll still line up to buy it. Fuck that whip. The best dope makes the most money." He got up and returned the pen to the lady at the desk.

I watched him, big, strong, and looking like nothing could stand in his way. Something did, though. He was here.

When he returned, it seemed as if he was reading my mind. "The most important thing, keep your business to yourself. No matter how much shit you move, who you sell to, never let nobody but your crew know what's going on. Work through other people. They never caught me with no dope, or got me on tape. The feds work through snitches. Keep your eyes open. Muthafuckas will give you up. Hide your dope and money. Some nigga can say he bought ten birds from you on such-and-such a day, and if they can get another one to tell the same lie, you can be charged with conspiracy. My lawyers are still fighting this shit, but they won't win. The deck is stacked.

"Now go over there and buy me a burger from the machine and heat it up. A Dr. Pepper too."

After asking Jas what she wanted, I did what he said. It took about ten minutes, and when I got back, him and Jas were talking quietly. I gave them their food, and we sat and talked until visitation was over at 2:45.

As we got up to leave, Big George said, "Tell your momma I said to give you the key." He turned and walked through the door.

As we were getting in the car, Jas said, "I like your old man. He's cool."

"What were you two talking about?"

"He told me how to help you. Also, he told me why you was scared of me." She gave a little smile.

"You told him—"

"I didn't tell him nothing. He told me. He said not to tell you what he said to do, and I ain't."

I was a little pissed off as we drove back to Houston mostly in silence.

Chapter Eleven

The three days until Wednesday were busier than hell. I didn't sell any of the dope we had. The first thing I did was look for a place for Jasmine. After looking at a few places we got from the paper, I settled for a detached two-bedroom condo in Bear Creek.

Forty-third Avenue turns into Clay Road a few blocks from Mama's house. Continuing west, across Gessner, Beltway 8, and Highway 6 is the area called Bear Creek, a nice neighborhood, not densely populated, with mostly mid-range houses and fairly expensive apartments.

I had Jas take out lease for a year, and pay the first six months up front. That was almost six grand. Furnishing it cost another nine. We were down to twelve thousand dollars and the dope.

Wednesday afternoon, I called the number and asked for José.

Before I could identify myself, the voice said, "You Big George's son, right?" The English was perfect, with just a trace of an accent.

"Yeah."

"Meet me in one hour at Meyerland Plaza, in front of J. C. Penney's. I'm in a black BMW. Come alone."

"Okay. But I've got my cousin with me. Big George's nephew. He's all right."

A moment's silence. "Just him then." He hung up.

Vic and I drove around to the West Loop and headed south toward the Jewish neighborhood of Meyerland. Naturally, we were strapped. I drove into the mall. Two rows back from Penney's door sat a black BMW with a man in it. I parked next to him.

The guy got out and walked over to my window. "I'm José."

"My name is Chris, and this is my cousin, Victor."

"Your papa is good people. He don't talk at all. This is why they give him so much time. He wrote me saying you need help, that you just like him. I hope this is true." He handed me a slip of paper. "Drive to this place now. I will meet you there." He got back into his car and drove off.

I opened the note to find directions to a house in Stafford, a small township next to Missouri City. I knew I could be there in twenty minutes. We drove the short distance down South Post Oak to Main. Turning right, we went out S. Main into Fort Bend County.

We didn't have any trouble finding the place. José was sitting on the trunk of his BMW, which was parked in the driveway of a white ranch-style house with black trim. "Come inside," he said. "Never come here without me. *¿Comprende?*"

I nodded, and Vic and I followed him in.

There was a minimum of furniture in the living room he led us through. In the kitchen, two Hispanic men stood near the sink. On the table was a black gym bag, and a larger duffle bag.

"Sit. We will talk."

We sat. I didn't know about my cousin, but I was a little nervous. Once I got involved with these people, there was no turning back. This first transaction was the most important, as far as I was concerned. I needn't have worried.

"This is for you. Ten kilos of the highest quality cocaine. One hundred thousand dollars cash. There is no charge. Your papa had this coming. In the future, you will pay twelve thousand dollars per kilo, but you must buy at least ten each time you come. I do not cut my supply. Your papa sold good rock, so he did not cut his either. Do you understand?"

"Yes. When I'm ready to re-up, do I use the same number, and will I deal only with you?"

"Yes to both. Now, I have a business opportunity for you. Also, a chance to help me with a small problem. You can say no, with no hard feelings. We"—He waved a hand to include the men by the sink—"are from Colombia. This part of town is ours. A group of Mexicans are moving in on us. They have set up a few miles from here. I could handle the problem, but it would start a conflict. Whoever takes them out will get both money and product. Are you interested?"

My mind quickly went over the situation. It was a test. At the same time, we could use the boost that the jack would give us. It would save time executing my plan. "We will handle your problem for you. When would you like it done?"

"Friday would be a good time. There will be three, maybe four, people in the house, one outside. You know what must be done."

"We can handle it. Do you know where Park Ten is?"

José nodded.

"There is a Charlie's Hamburger on Highway 6 just south of the I-10. Can you meet me there tomorrow morning at eight? I need to see the place. In the morning would be best."

He smiled. He knew just what I meant. I wanted to case the place at a time when the people inside would most likely be asleep, and when the usual morning activity of the street would help cover us. I also wanted him to know that we might be a couple of young niggas, but we damn sure weren't crash dummies.

"I will be there. You are indeed your father's son. He was always thinking. I look forward to our doing business." Standing, he motioned to one of the men. "Luis will show you how to cook the powder for maximum potency. When you are satisfied that you've got it, you can go. I'll see you in the morning."

He left, and we stayed another hour. The big difference in the cooking process was that you had to use a deep enough container to boil the dope. That ensured that all the impurities were gone. The amount of baking soda used, and the cooling process were the same. It came back hard, and one lick really numbed your tongue.

When we were done, we nodded to Luis and Francisco, grabbed the bags, and left.

I took the beltway all the way to Clay Road.

Vic was excited. "You know how much money we got already, cuz?"

"The twelve birds will get us over two hundred thousand if we move them as stones. Plus, there's the cash. No telling what we'll get Friday."

That thought sobered us both.

José's little test involved going in, killing everybody there, and jacking for the money and dope. Were we really ready for this? Killing Herman and his boys had been one thing. That was personal and necessary for my and Jasmine's safety. But this was some real gangster shit. Once I took this step, I was totally committed to the life. Was I ready? Damn right!

"We need more than me, you, and Boar Hog. After we drop this off with Jas, we go to the hood."

The condo looked nice after Jasmine fixed it up. The door was steel, as was the frame, and was painted to look like wood. Jas had followed all my instructions.

I gave her the small bag to put in the safe. Then I took the dope to the closet in the second bedroom.

I didn't go into detail, but I told her we had to go to Acres Home. On the way I would use the key I had gotten from Mama.

Chapter Twelve

The key was to a self-storage unit in a place just off Magnum and Highway 290. Mama was surprised when I'd asked her for it.

She sighed, looked into my eyes for a long time, and gave it to me. "Just be careful, baby."

I felt a twinge of guilt. Now she had to know that I was following in my father's footsteps. If only she knew the truth. "I will, Mama."

When Vic and I pulled off the lock and opened the unit, it looked like it was full of junk and old furniture. We cleaned a path to the rear. There was a wall of metal shelves with oily cloth bundles on each one. I picked up one of the bundles at random and unwrapped it. I was looking at a machine pistol.

"Damn!" Vic said.

We opened a few others. It was a fucking arsenal—two

AK-47's, three .45 automatics, two sawed-off 12-gauge shotguns, and a couple of other pistols. And a metal footlocker on the bottom shelf held an assortment of ammunition.

"Unc was ready for a war," Vic muttered.

I took an AK, the MP5, and both shotguns, and put them in my truck, and Vic got the ammo for them.

We headed for Boar Hog's house. When we went inside, I told him to empty the place. Even Lucille. I ran down my visit to José to him.

"We're gonna need a couple more men. You got anybody in mind?"

"Yeah. This here is my street. Most of the youngsters out there selling work for Fred Jackson. I figure we could start here. Two young brothers, Freddie and Frank Collier, would be good. They're jackers anyway, an' they ain't scared of nothin'. Me and yo' daddy put in some work with them before. You want me to, I'll go get 'em right now."

"Do it."

A few minutes later Boar Hog came back with two young men and made the introductions. Freddie was slim and dark-skinned. He looked to be about twenty-five. His brother was short and stocky, brown-skinned, with reddish hair cut short.

"I got a job to do. We gonna take down some Mexicans on the other side of town. Five of them in a house. We hit it Friday, late. You want in, we split all the cash we get. I keep all the dope, plus my one-fifth of the cash. Boar says you two get down. You in?"

"You sho there be enough money to make it worthwhile?"

"If there ain't, then I'll make up the difference myself."

Frank asked. "Ain't you Big George's son?"

"Yeah. So what?"

"So we in. Your daddy was all right with us. When you want us ready?"

"Be here Friday at midnight. The five of us are it. Nobody knows about this but us. We're gonna do it, get the shit, and get out."

"We'll be here."

I took Boar Hog outside behind them. I pulled him over to the truck, flipped back the tarp, and showed him the guns.

"Let's put them in my room. I keep it locked, and none of them hoes gonna go in there."

After we did that, I took Boar and Vic up to the Verizon Wireless store on Antoine and got them new cell phones. Then we went to the lot on Pinemont and bought a used Taurus in Vic's name. Vic was going to stay over at Boar Hog's tonight, so he could learn some more about The Four-Four. I told them to ring me at noon tomorrow.

When I made it back to Bear Creek, it was dark. Jas was watching TV. She jumped up to fix me some food.

She waited until I was done eating to ask, "What's wrong?"

I told her the whole deal. I expected her to try and

talk me out of it, like most women would have, but she surprised me.

"I can see where you damn near gotta do it, if you want to keep doing business with José. Just be careful."

I looked over at her. All of a sudden I wanted to make love to her. Badly. She must have noticed the look in my eyes.

"You don't look scared no more. Before you get all worked up, I'm just coming off my period. Please, let's wait until tomorrow night. I want it to be right our first time." She reached over and grabbed my dick. "I can still help with that."

My first thought was selfish. I could go wait on Linda to get off and fuck her down. Looking at Jas, though, I felt guilty. It wasn't her fault we weren't sleeping together, it was mine. Damn near every man I knew in my age group spent most of their time either trying to, or actually getting laid. I was guilty of that myself quite often.

Where I figured I differed was, I took to heart something my daddy told me when I was about fourteen years old and just beginning to become obsessed with sex. He said, "Boy, don't let your dick run your life. It can fuck you up and get you in more trouble than twenty pissed-off niggers. Take care of business first. You'll appreciate the sex a lot more, and it won't control you." My daddy's word was gospel to me. I always tried to remember and act on the things he taught me.

Right now, though, I wanted Jasmine, and the hell

with anything else. I pulled her to me, and we made out right there on the sofa.

She sucked me off like before then brought herself, while I sucked her breasts and rubbed that big, beautiful ass. She wouldn't let me touch her pussy.

I could smell that her time was upon her, but I didn't give a shit.

As we dozed off, she whispered, "Tomorrow."

The neighborhood Jose took me to the next morning was more like the country than the city. I thought we were still in Stafford, but I wasn't sure. The house he showed me was in a little cul-de-sac with two vacant lots on either side. The nearest house to it was on the street behind, which was about eighty yards away, and most of the area consisted of open fields.

"Every night, there's a car parked at the end of the driveway," José said. "Somebody will be in it. They watch out for the house. Inside, there is a closet in the front room. That's where the dope is. The money will be in the back bedroom. There will be four men. They don't allow women or strangers here."

"Sounds like you've been inside."

"I have. I tried to work this problem out."

I didn't pry further. "We'll do it about two or three a.m. How many bedrooms?"

"Three. The back one is empty. No furniture. I think one man sleeps in the front room, the others, in the bedrooms. I will draw you a picture."

We turned around in the circle at the end of the street.

Anyway I looked at it, we would have to come on foot. I would bring Vic and Boar back through here this afternoon, but a plan was already forming in my mind.

"When it's done, I'll call you. I won't say much, but you'll know."

After I took him back to his car, I had time to kill, so I went back to Bear Creek. I grabbed Jas when I came in the door and gave her a long kiss, running my hands over her ass. "Tonight. Right now, it's time to put you to work. You're going to learn how to cook crack."

By the time Vic called at noon, we had done two kilos, and she had it figured out. The table was covered with slabs drying on paper towels. I told Vic to bring Boar Hog, and they arrived thirty minutes later.

Boar Hog took a pencil and a piece of tinfoil and made a homemade pipe. He put a small chunk of rock on it and lit up. "Ooh shit! That's the lick! This is the kind of dope that made your old man rich."

"Us too, I hope. Let's ride."

Vic drove, and Boar rode shotgun, as I directed them from the back seat of the Taurus. We drove the streets on either side of the cul-de-sac, and finally drove by the place itself.

Boar Hog didn't seem worried at all. "It ain't perfect, but it ain't hopeless neither. We can do it."

"Bo, I want you to come around from behind the

house and wait behind that bush on the corner. When the shooting starts, take out the guy in the car. Vic will take one bedroom window, and Frank the other. Both with shotguns, me and Freddie will go in the back door. We'll take the guy in the front room, and anybody that makes it out of the bedrooms. Bo, when you do the guard out front, come in the front door and get the dope. I'll get the money. Vic, you and the Colliers go through the other rooms real quick. Then we burn off."

They both agreed. "All right, drop me off, and I'll grab Jasmine. We'll go to The Four-Four, sell a little rock, and draw it up for Freddie and Frank."

At the condo, I broke off half a slab, wrapped it up, and Jasmine and I went to Acres Home. I had her drop me off on Bethune, and she took the Acura to her momma's house.

Inside Boar Hog's, I called for a plate and blade to cut up the dope. As I did, I couldn't help but think of Big George. How many times as a little boy had I watched him do this?

Each slab we cooked up was done in a shallow Pyrex baking dish and would yield just over half a kilo, about eighteen ounces. The way Big George did it was the way I considered best. He cut fifty stones from each ounce of crack. Of course, this made for some really large rocks, each one being more than twice the size a customer would expect from a good twenty-dollar stone.

The guys slinging the rocks bought them (or, more likely, had them fronted to them) at twenty per stone. For each ounce, our end was $1000. The slingers cut the rocks in half, thereby receiving two grand per ounce. They received as much money as we did per ounce, but their risk was much greater. Our workers could each earn eight, ten grand a week. We earned that, times the number of workers we had.

My plan was to have them all. The twelve keys we had already, plus whatever we got from the jack, would be our start. We had our work cut out for us. Besides an unlimited supply of powder, we needed to take and hold the territory that would provide the number of workers to earn at least a million dollars a week on our end.

I had done the math. Vic, Bo, and maybe the Colliers would all be paid out of what the workers brought us, and they would earn their money. It all started here with these nine ounces.

It was time to bag them up, but first things first. "Lucille!" I yelled.

She must have been right outside the door.

I handed her a handful of the small pebbles and shake leftover from the cutting. "You and your girlfriends try this out, and tell me what you think."

"Thanks, Chris." She looked over at Vic. "Carolyn was by here looking for you." Carolyn was one of Lucille's dope fiend friends.

After sending Boar for the Colliers, I turned to my cousin and said, "Tell me you ain't fucking these chickenheads. Your dick is gonna fall off. Be cool, and we'll go to the club this weekend. Jas will hook you up."

"Don't knock it till you try it, cuz. Carolyn's a vacuum

cleaner. Besides, I'm scared that if I hang around with you and Jas, I might catch that deadly disease you got."

"What the fuck you talking about, boy?"

"Play crazy if you want. You can't bullshit me. I know you. You got it bad, and I don't want it. I'll stick to Carolyn the Hoover."

I laughed and shook my head. I really didn't want to go there with him.

Lucille knocked on the door. Her mouth was twisted, and her nipples stood out like thumbs against her thin shirt.

"Shit, Chris. That shit's the truth. Every pussy in there is soaking wet. Got some more? Them bitches ready to get naked and rape you for some of that shit."

"Tell them hoes to go to work. They bring us enough sales, and I'll hook 'em up."

Boar Hog walked in with Freddie and Frank behind him.

I took out the map I'd re-drawn and went over the plan with them.

Freddie said, "Bo and whoever else stays outside better not come in until the shooting stops an' we open the door. Don't want them to get shot by mistake. Everything in that house is gonna get blasted, 'cept us."

"You're right." I looked up at him. "Good lookin' out." I showed them the dope. "We're gonna start slinging some major weight. You guys want to help?"

Frank said, "Fred ain't gonna like that."

"Fuck Fred! This is the best shit in Houston. Fred's

got a problem with me, we can settle it. Far as I'm concerned, I'm just taking over my old man's action."

"That's a lot of action."

"An' I'm gonna get it all back, and more. You with me?"

"Shit, lil' King, we already doin' business together. Besides, Big George was the best. I think we'll ride."

I handed each of them a Ziploc bag. "There's a hundred and fifty stones in each bag. Each of you bring my cousin three grand." I explained to them how the money worked. The deal I gave them was more than fair. "It's just like Big George used to do it. Everybody gets to eat."

They both nodded.

"When we do our job tomorrow, I'll sit down with you and run down how we're gonna take off. This shit is so good, it will lock up the trade. I got a plan that's gonna make us all richer than you can believe. Just pack fair, an' you got it made. I'll meet you here tomorrow night. Right now we need to get this shit to the dopeheads, so word gets out."

After the Colliers left, I turned to Boar and Vic. "There's another hundred and fifty stones here. Same thing—Bring six grand, cut it up, and move it through Lucille and them hoes. Don't let them freaks beat you. Don't worry about your cut. We all get paid out of the total take. That means you got to trust me like I'm trusting you."

"Boy, yo' daddy must have spit you out. I said I was down."

Vic said, "I know you wasn't talking to me about trustin' you, cuz."

"Naw. Bo either, really. I just want it all on the table between us. And, Bo, watch out for 'Horny Harry' here. Don't let Carolyn kill him."

Bo and I laughed as Vic flipped us the bird.

I turned at the door. "Don't mix it up with Fred Jackson, if you can help it. Tell him he needs to see me. Big George said he was a good, honest worker for him. There's enough of them others that we will have to bust up."

I walked over to Miss Jennings's house and visited with her for a while.

Then I took the path to the other end of Parkes Street. When I came out of the woods, I could see the Acura parked at Jasmine's mother's house.

I knocked on the door and took the ribbing from her sisters and mom about Jas and me.

Finally I turned to Jas. "You ready?"

She looked at me. She knew I was talking about more than just going home. "I'm ready if you are."

For some reason her momma found that funny as hell. I could still hear her laughing as we got in the car.

Chapter Thirteen

When we got inside the condo, Jasmine turned to me. "I'm going to shower. Don't come in until you hear the water running."

I didn't know what the problem was, but I went along. I was horny, and it was time. I had wanted her little ass since I was six. Even before I knew what my dick was for.

I stacked some of my parents' old-school love songs into the CD changer. Big George was always listening to Prince, Keith Sweat, the Isleys, and bragging to me about how much pussy he got off that music when he was young. Of course, Mama was never around while he thumped his chest.

I smiled at this thought while I put an ice bucket and some Bristol Cream—Yuck! the things we do for love, or sex, anyway—on the nightstand and went to join Jas.

When I saw the strawberry douche box in the garbage

can, I knew why she made me wait. I opened the stall door. This was the first time I had seen her completely naked in good light. *Damn!* I thought.

She opened her eyes in the spray and looked at me. Even though Jas was 5-6, her legs looked long and sleek, and her hips flared to a small waist. The breasts were full, and looking bigger than they ought to be in proportion to the rest of her body. Her ass was a work of art, not large enough to be gross, but bigger than it seemed, though natural for her size. Altogether, she was a knockout.

I stood there like a zombie.

"Close your mouth, boy, and let's get you clean. I been waiting thirteen years for this."

That broke the spell. I had to laugh. That was exactly what I had been thinking earlier.

I took her into my arms. By the time we broke the kiss, we were both on fire. The water cascaded around us as I reveled in the feel of her hot flesh beneath my hands. In no hurry, we washed each other slowly. Jas was panting with desire, and I was so hard, it hurt. The toweling was hurried.

Still half-wet, we ran to the bed. Jas tried to grab my dick, but I held her off. I lay her down and knelt between her legs.

"Hurry, Chris. I want it so bad."

As much as I ached to ram my dick into her, I made myself wait. If what she'd said was true, she hadn't had a whole lot of sex. I knew that I was bigger than average, and I didn't want to hurt her. I bent and tasted her.

Her thighs clamped themselves around my ears, and she moaned.

I cupped her ass to pull her closer. Her juices flowed from her as I tongued her slit. I took the small, erect bud at the top and squeezed it between my lips.

"Oh! Oh! I'm coming, baby!" Ass cheeks flexing, she thrashed beneath me.

I couldn't wait any longer. Jas was still, trembling and moaning when I started to push into her. Her eyes opened wide. Man, she was tight!

"Does it hurt?"

"No. Yes. A little. It's all right. Please don't stop!"

Inch by inch, I went in. With slow, gentle strokes, I eased further until three-quarters of my length was inside her. It took all my self-control not to move. I let her get accustomed to me. She started to rotate her hips slowly. I could feel her pussy getting hotter, wetter, and looser around me.

When she started to raise her hips from the bed, I knew she was ready. I pushed it all in.

"Aaah, yes," she moaned as I filled her up.

Now, I began to stroke her. It felt like heaven as we rocked in perfect rhythm.

She was taking it all now, and pushing her pelvis against mine for more. "Oh, Chris. Baby, I'm going to come again."

I knew what I really wanted. When I pulled all the way out of her, she gasped in protest. I flipped her over onto her knees and pushed into her from behind.

That big, sweet ass pushing into my groin sent me

over. I began to hit her hard, our bodies slamming together with enough force to flatten her butt on each stroke. She grunted each time I went in.

Just as I felt her pussy start to spasm, I shot my seed into her with a groan of my own, and she screamed my name.

I laid her down on her face, cupping her breasts as her hips pulled the last of my juice from me. I rolled off her, and she turned over into my arms.

We didn't need words, because it was special for both of us. We kept running our hands over each other's bodies until the need built again.

This time she straddled me and slowly lowered herself onto my pole. Soon she was riding me with abandon. I grabbed her hips and thrust upwards until I exploded. We slept.

When I woke up, Jas was stroking my morning hard-on with both hands. The scent of her and our lovemaking filled the room.

"Boy, you too much. My little pussy is sore." She smiled as she bent and sucked me dry.

She went to draw a bath, and when she was done, I showered.

At the breakfast table, in between shit-eating grins at each other, I asked her, "What kind of business do you want to buy, ma? We already started slinging the dope. After tonight, I'm really going to get into it."

"I saw an empty storefront at T. C. Jester and Little

York, up by the Stop-N-Shop. You know, right next to the wig place?"

I nodded.

"I was thinking, What if I opened a nail shop—manicures, pedicures, make-up and stuff—and we got your mom to open a beauty shop where the wig place is?"

I thought about it. This was a good idea. Like Daddy said, we needed a way to wash some of our money. Two businesses were better than one. Besides the legitimate money they would make, I could put enough of our drug money through their books to justify the way we would be living. Looking back, I can see neither of us had any idea of the kind of money we were talking about. Not even Daddy.

"That's a good idea. Check it out. We've got the money to lease the space and buy the equipment, but I want y'all to get an SBA or bank loan anyway. This has got to look totally legit. Mama's got an old customer who is a lawyer. Get her to help. Use the money you need from the safe."

Jasmine's eyes lit up. She looked so happy. I would look back later and remember the joy, hope, and even love that was on her face right now.

"What?"

"Remember when I told you not to stick that thing of yours in me until you wasn't scared no more? Well, you did, and you did it good. We're in this business thing together. But this is something else. I ain't gonna worry you about shit like love and marriage. As long as you fucking me though, you better act like you got some sense. I ain't no ho. Ain't never been no ho. You find some bitch you like better than me, come tell me. We can split the money. I'll get your shit out of my name, and we can still be friends. I'm being straight with you, and all I'm asking is that you be straight with me."

I was more than a little hurt by what she said. In my heart I was feeling her a lot. She was more than just a piece of pussy to me. I guess I wanted it both ways. I wanted her to be my woman, for us to really be together like Big George and Mama, without having to lock myself into a one-woman corner. She was a lot smarter than me, even then. I just hadn't figured it out yet.

"So what we got here is a business relationship and a sexual relationship?"

"That's not what I said. I said I wouldn't nag you about love and marriage. I didn't say I didn't want it." She got up and left the table.

I sat there for a while. I could see that she was about to cry.

I knew the deal. Jas was a bad-ass woman. I just didn't know if I was ready for the commitment that I sensed she really wanted. Even as I was making the decision to leave things the way they were, I was moving into the bedroom, where she sat red-eyed and tearful.

I went to her and pulled her into my arms. "Jas, hush, baby. I have wanted nobody but you since we were kids. You are the finest, most beautiful, sexiest, and smartest woman I know. Don't cry. Not over me. I only know that, right now, I got to grind. I'm gonna stack so much paper, they can't possibly take enough to hurt me. When Big George gets home, his set is gonna be ready for him. I want you to know that I want you. I need you. Believe that. Daddy told me a long time not to make promises I couldn't keep. That's all that's holding me back. Just give me a little time."

She wrapped her arms around me and kissed me hard, and I stroked her and played with her, and left her laughing again.

Then I went to plan some killings.

green duffle bag. I sat it on the bed and looked inside—money. Another check of the room turned up nothing, so I left.

Vic and Boar Hog both had bags in their hands as I returned to the front room. "Bricks," Boar Hog said.

"Let's go."

We all rushed out the back door and stumbled across the field. When we got to the vehicles, we threw the guns and the dope into the trunk of Vic's car. Boar Hog got behind the wheel. Vic, holding the duffle I'd found, got into the passenger seat of my truck.

We drove back to Highway 90, ran up to Beltway 8, and took the expressway. Three toll booths later, we were cruising east on West Little York, headed back to Acres Home.

It was 3:40 when we got to Boar Hog's house. Once there, we took everything into his room.

The money came to just over five hundred thousand dollars. Vic and Freddie split it five ways, giving each of us about a hundred grand.

While they did this, I called Jose's number on my cell. "It's done." I hung up. "Cuz, you coming with me. Grab one of those bags. I'll see the rest of you here later. It went good. We were lucky. Now it's time for us to go to work." I picked up the other bag of dope, and we walked out.

As we drove back down Little York toward Bear Creek, Vic said, "Man, cuz, what a rush! We did it! Tell the truth, now—This is me—Wasn't you scared?"

Chapter Fourteen

It was 2:30 in the morning when we hit the Mexicans. The sky was overcast, and it was dark as shit in the field behind the house, which was still and quiet. We'd left the Taurus and my truck on the street behind the cul-de-sac.

The going was slow until we reached the backyard. Gloved and masked, we probably looked just like the jackers we were. I pointed to the left, and Boar Hog started off.

I gave him a few minutes. If the guy out front wasn't there, or not in the car, he would come and tell us. When he didn't come back, I pointed to the right.

The bedroom Frank Collier would take was at the right rear window. Frank would spray his room. Vic would take the front, near the middle. He would start by pumping shotgun rounds into his window. Boar Hog would do his guy.

Me and Freddie moved to the back door. If all the Mexicans were where they were supposed to be, it should work. If not, we might be fucked.

The wait seemed to be forever. My heart was thudding in my chest as I switched the Calico to my left hand and pulled the .357. I wanted that door open quick, and this cannon would put a hole through an engine block.

Even though I was waiting for it, when the first shotgun blast came, I jumped. Then all hell broke loose. It sounded like a war movie, only louder.

I put the Magnum close to the knob and pulled the trigger, and Freddie kicked at the door till it swung open. We were in.

Freddie ran through the kitchen and started spraying the living room with the AK.

The guy must have been lying on the couch, because when I came up beside Freddie, I could see his bare feet scrambling on the floor as he moved around the far end. I ripped off six or seven rounds with the Calico.

Then I raised the .357. The roar was tremendous. I saw blood shoot up as the round tore a fist-size hole into the arm of the sofa, and into the guy behind it.

I pointed down the hall, and Freddie and I turned to face the dark opening. I heard a sound as someone tried to open the door in the middle. I put two rounds through the door and the wall next to it.

I heard a shotgun boom again.

"Hey, guys. It's us."

We whipped around as Boar Hog and Frank into the living room. Freddie hit the light switc

I pointed down the hall, and walked to the fr as the others made their way slowly toward rooms. "Vic! Come on."

My cousin stepped in, holding his shotgun ac chest. His breathing was rapid, but his eyes sh excitement.

When I turned back to the hall, Boar Hog door open, and Freddie the other. Frank stoo middle with his shotgun.

"Check the front closet."

Vic went to do so.

I walked down the hall, easing around Frank into the room behind the farthest door. As I pa other bedrooms, I barely took in the bloody shotgun blasts had caused.

I pushed the final door open. The guy in ther up. The closet had a sliding door, and that's wh decided to take cover. Problem was, he had to door to see. If he had waited a few more sec might have gotten me. The slight sound of th door sliding on its track was enough to alert m pered the door from side to side with the Calic heard a grunt and a thud.

The guys came running.

"Check the other rooms. We got to get out of walked to the closet and slowly slid the door Mexican dude with long hair and holding an slumped on the floor. After rolling the body out,

I looked over at him. “Slick, I was scared shitless, but we had it to do. You know what scares me more?”

This was my boy. From the crib. Except my parents, there was no human being who I was closer to, so I felt I could say this to him.

“No. What?”

“That I really didn’t feel anything when I blew those guys away. They were between me and what I wanted. Herman and his boys over in the hood, well, that was personal, as well as self-defense. This was business. Make no mistake about it, Slick, I’m gonna do what I said. I’m headed to the top of this game. All the way.”

We rode for a while in silence.

I could see Vic thinking about what I’d said. Finally, he spoke. “I believe you. And you know, I got yo’ back.”

That was all I needed to hear.

I was in a good mood when we got to the condo. I kissed Jasmine and gave her the hundred gees. We pulled the bricks out of the bags and stacked them on the kitchen table. There were fifty kilos.

Vic grabbed Jas and hugged her. “We’re rich!”

They were both still smiling when I took my knife and cut into one of the bricks.

“Shit!”

“What’s wrong, baby?”

I didn’t answer. I took a Pyrex measuring cup from the cabinet. Weighing out one half-ounce, I dumped it in with a pinch of baking soda. I added a little water and put it on the stove to boil. When the water was mostly clear, I used a potholder to hold the cup while I dripped cold water in and rotated it.

When the dope came together and got hard, I dumped it out and put it on the scale. It weighed right at one-quarter ounce. "This shit is cut to hell. At least a fifty. We'll lose at least half of it, unless we want to sell that same bullshit as everyone else."

"Maybe not, cuz."

I turned to Vic, my jaws tight. "What the hell you mean?"

"You know I worked shipping and receiving at the Medical Center. Once a month they get a shipment from Costa Pharmaceuticals. Next to Merck, they're the biggest ones out there. One of the things they order is cocaine hydrochloride. Know what that is?"

I had an idea. "You don't mean to tell me—"

"Yep. Pharmaceutical cocaine. The only hundred percent pure cocaine you can get. Hell, it may be even more powerful than the natural shit. I ain't no chemist and shit, but you pick up things. They use it for anesthesia and some shit to do with heart patients. A little of that stuff in each bird would make this shit kick-ass."

"What does it look like?"

"It comes in a big bottle. About five pounds in each jar. Got a big skull and crossbones on it sayin', 'DANGER! POISON! COCAINE HYDROCHLORIDE USP."

"And you can get us a bottle of this shit from the Medical Center?"

"No way, man. After we receive it, shit's under lock and key, cameras, guards, the whole works. UTMB receives medical supplies for the whole Medical Center. They escort all the dangerous drugs straight upstairs."

"Then why did you bring it up, if we can't get it?"

"I didn't say we can't get it. Just not from the Medical Center. You know me, I fuck with everybody. I know the driver who delivers it, his route, everything. We can jack it."

I stood stunned for a minute. Then I grabbed him and kissed him on the forehead. "You slick muthafucka! Let's do it!"

Vic wiped his head. "Yuck! Let me find out you done gone funny on me, boy. I'm-a tell Aunt Dot."

I looked at Jas.

"Naw, cuz, he definitely ain't funny."

"Then the muthafucka just weird then."

We all broke up with laughter.

"You just made this weird muthafucka a millionaire. We got what, baby?"

Jas didn't hesitate. "With what you got from Herman, José, and that lick y'all hit, right at sixty-two kilos of dope, and one hundred twenty thousand dollars cash."

Vic let out a low whistle. "Damn, *C*, you been busy. Won't you take my money and put with the rest? Bo and the Colliers will have the money from the stones tomorrow. The way you explained the cash flow ought to work."

"What do you mean?" Jasmine asked.

I quickly explained the way I would move the dope and collect the money. With this much to start with, I began to see a way for it to really work. The key was to keep the best dope, and plenty of it. There was gonna be some bloodshed for sure. Niggers weren't going to give up their territory without a fight. We'd just have to take it to them.

Jas said, "No. Everything you say is true, but there is a better way to handle the finances. You got Vic, Boar Hog, the two Colliers, and us. Nobody in that group needs to be selling rock to make their money. If every ounce of rock nets a thousand dollars, and the workers are already paid, then that grand's got to pay the crew.

"Why don't you take fifty percent for us, twenty for Vic, and the other thirty can be split three ways between Boar Hog and the Colliers. Your cousin is family, and he is going to eventually have to oversee a lot of people. The split has to be after expenses, but it's fair, and it allows you to predict and control income. What do you think?"

Before I could answer, Vic said, "I think you ought to dump this chump and marry me."

"Shut up, trick. Go marry the vacuum cleaner. This one is mine."

From the middle of a big smile, Jas said, "Vacuum cleaner? Please tell me he's not talking about Carolyn?" Then she really started to laugh.

Vic mumbled, "I don't care what y'all say. The girl's got skills."

"Yeah, and if you lucky, that's all she got. Say, baby, that's pretty good, what you said about the split. I was wondering what was the best way to do it. For a square lady, you sure seem to know a lot about the game."

"Who said I was a square? I grew up in dope central. Just because I didn't get involved till we got together don't mean I kept my eyes closed. You think I wasn't tempted by the money? I just wasn't gonna play myself like that."

I had a lot more to ask, but I didn't think this conversation was for Vic's ears, even though he was my boy.

"Anyway, I like what you said. Sound okay to you, Slick?"

"You know it. Mama got skills. Got any more at home like you?"

Jas and I looked at each other and laughed.

"Yeah. I got two sisters, and if you ever piss me off, I'm gonna hook you up."

"What? She look like Godzilla or something?"

"Nah. She looks just like me, one of 'em anyway. Trust me, though, you don't wanna go there. Chenise is my sister and I love her, but the girl is out there bad."

Vic started to say something, but stopped. I could see his mind working. He would pump me about Jas's sister later.

We sat around and talked for another hour. Then, after installing Vic in the spare bedroom, we went to bed.

Chapter Fifteen

Jas had already talked to Mama about her proposal, so they were going to talk to the lawyer and look at the building this morning. We all got a late start.

After going to bed, I was still amped from the hit, and from the sure knowledge that somehow I'd landed that one-in-a-million woman that would be down for a brother in every way. Such thoughts naturally made me hard, but surprisingly, Jas was a little embarrassed to do it with someone else only a wall away. I thought this was an endearing trait, but I had a hard dick, and she was my woman, so I wasn't trying to hear that shit.

The result was a long, slow fuck.

We lay on our sides, spooning. I prodded her fine ass with my hard dick, and she wiggled around until it slipped in. Embarrassed or not, she was wet and ready. I reached around her and held her breasts in my hands as she pushed her soft ass back against me. We went on this way for the better part of an hour.

I lost track of how many times she came. Each time her pussy tightened around me and she stuck her hand in her mouth to stifle her moans, I just got harder. When I passed out, I was still pumping slowly in and out of her.

When I woke up, it was after eleven. I shook Vic up and gave him a toothbrush and let him wash up. Then I sent him to the Medical Center in my truck. I called Mama and told her Jas would be by to pick her up in a couple of hours.

Jasmine woke up as I was gently washing her with a warm cloth. My dick was so hard, it hurt. When I replaced the cloth with my lips, she started to moan.

Suddenly she froze. “Chris, the door.”

Once I assured her that Vic was gone, and I had called Mama, she relaxed. I rose to my knees and entered her, trying to take my time and enjoy the pleasant sensation of her velvety box caressing my dick. I couldn’t take it, though.

I reached down, grabbed her hips, and pulled her to me hard, slamming into her with all my might.

“Oh shit! Chris!”

I threw her legs over my shoulders and “gorilla fucked” her long, hard, and fast.

I felt my balls start to tighten, and my dick swell even more. Then her thighs locked around my neck and started to tremble. We came violently together for what seemed like forever. I rolled over, and we lay side by side, both of us panting.

"Damn, boy. You tryin' to kill a bitch."

"Shit, I'm the one who can't breathe."

"I can't walk. You're gonna have to carry me to the shower, and bathe me too."

By the time she dropped me at Boar Hog's, there was just enough time for her to get Mama and make the lawyer's. When I walked into the house without knocking, my good mood changed pretty quickly. The moment I stepped into his bedroom, I knew he'd fucked up.

The door to his room was open, and the first thing I saw was Lucille's hairy pussy. She was spread-eagled on the bed, pipe in hand. Her ribs were starting to show, and she was too thin. Once again I was struck with the thought that, if she left that shit alone and put on a few pounds, she would be a fine-looking woman.

I slapped her leg. "Lucille! Lucille!"

"Who? Oh, Chris. Boar Hog will be right back. He went to get some cigarettes."

"Get up, girl, and put some clothes on. I want to talk to you." I walked back outside and sat on the steps.

This could fuck up all my plans. Maybe I should just kick her crackhead ass and send her packing, but I kind of needed her right now. I needed Boar sober even more. When I heard Lucille walking through the house I called, "Come out here."

She walked out and stood in front of me.

"I'm only gonna tell you this once. Boar Hog has been good to you. Why you wanna fuck him up? The only way he's gonna stay off that shit is if you help him."

"But we got all the money from that dope."

"Don't bullshit me. If you use his money to buy it, then where's his profit? We can all get paid. Big. If you fuck up Boar Hog, then you're fucking me over. I don't think you wanna do that."

"No, I never would. I know what happens when people fuck you over." She must have read my mind, or maybe it was just the look on my face. "Boar don' say nothin' about y'all's business. You know how it is out here. Everybody know that Herman had it in for you, an' all of a sudden, him an' his boys turn up dead. Don' take no genius."

I left that one alone. "Lucille, why don't you get off that shit? Boar Hog is gonna get paid, even if I have to take him away from here and keep him with me. You're a good-looking woman. He needs you. Shit, I need you. We could all be rich."

"I'll try, Chris. I really will."

"Don't try. Do it. Tell him I went to find Freddie and Frank. I'll be back." I looked at her. "Keep my bag here." I gave her the bag with the dope. I didn't say anything else, but she knew the deal. Fail this test, and I was through with her.

As I walked off around the house, my thoughts were churning. It was going to be hard to ride herd on Boar and Lucille. Nobody in their right mind would try to do the shit I was going to do with a couple of crackheads. Common sense said to cut them both loose.

On the other side of the equation was the fact that I knew Boar Hog was all the way down for whatever. And he was loyal. Plus, he already knew that I'd done several murders. And he knew about Jas's involvement. Truth was, if I dropped him, I would have to kill him. And Lucille. I made my decision. I liked the crusty old muthafucka. He was my Daddy's friend.

I would put Vic on point to make sure they stayed away from the pipe. If it continued to be a concern, then I could do something about it later. Right now, it was time to get things really started.

I found the Colliers at home and told them to meet me at Boar Hog's in thirty minutes.

When I walked back into his bedroom, Boar was sitting with a beer in his hand. He hung his head when he saw me.

"What's up, Bo?"

"I'm good, youngster. Say—"

I cut him off. "I'm-a be straight with you, Boar. You old school, an' I heard enough about you from my daddy to know that you real people. Not to mention the shit we done together. I need your help, I can't lie. More than that though, I need to know that I can trust you.

Crazy as it sounds, I know I can trust you with my life. But can I trust you with my money and my dope? Your pockets real fat now. If you want to take your ends an' party with your girl till it's gone, just say so. I'll even sell you the dope at a discount. If you want to keep your word an' help me re-build Big George's empire, I'll be glad. If you an' Lucille want to step, I ain't gonna be mad at you."

Boar Hog raised his head and looked me in the eye. His eyes were moist, but no tears fell. I could see the effort it took to restrain them. When Lucille took a step toward him, he warned her off with a look.

"Lil' King, you don't know much about me. There was a time, when I was not much older than you, when I was the coldest player in The Four-Four. I had it all—money, women, and respect. Made most of my money slingin' boy an' "teas & blues." My main woman was my common-law wife, Shirley. We had two of the prettiest little girls you ever seen, Rita and Felicia. Had a house over on Aruba in Lincoln City. One day, nigger from Fifth Ward tried to jack me. I busted a cap in his bitch ass. Thought that was the end of it. Two nights later, while I was up by Sear's ranch, two pussy muthafuckas from his hood firebombed my house. Shirley, Rita, and little C.C. were in the bed 'sleep. They all died. I went crazy. I got my shotgun and two pistols and went over there."

He pulled up his tee shirt. His skin had seven or eight of the shiny, dimpled scars that could only be bullet wounds.

"When I got out of the hospital, my people was already in the ground. At night, every time I closed my eyes, I could hear my babies screaming for their daddy. I started running dope just so I could sleep. You can figure the rest. I ain't tellin' you this so you will feel sorry fo' me. Don't need that.

"Yo' daddy came to town 'bout four years after this happened. By then I was a full-fledged junkie. He heard what had happened, an' without even knowing me, he came to see me, got me cleaned up, an' put me down with his crew.

"For a whole bunch of years, my life had a purpose. I did a lot of dirt, planted a bunch of suckers, but that's all part of the game. What yo' daddy did for me wasn't. And he never said a word, never acted like I owed him anything. When he got knocked, I lost my anchor. Can you understand that?"

Gripped by his story, I nodded.

"Well, youngster, now you come along an' give me a chance to not only stand up again, but to repay a debt. So, can you trust me to help you? Yeah, you can." Boar Hog looked over at Lucille.

"You gon' stay or go?"

"What you talkin' about? I ain't goin' nowhere."

"Then go get all the pipes and cookers and chunk that shit. Then go to S & P and get some food to cook. We got company comin', and it's gonna take a while."

Lucille left without a word.

I sat there a minute wondering what I could say in response to the story he'd just told me. Big George had never gone into any detail about his workers, and I hadn't known anything about Boar Hog's past. My gut told me that he was for real, though, and that I didn't have to worry about him anymore.

Chapter Sixteen

Frank and Freddie Collier came into the bedroom. We greeted each other, and Boar gave them a beer. After rehashing last night's action, I explained the financial arrangements that me, Vic, and Jas had discussed. They were all for the deal.

Vic walked in. When he was seated, I asked Frank if he had heard anything from Fred Jackson.

He reached into his pocket and handed me a bundle of money. "Fred pulled up and asked me about the dope. I told him I got it from you. He seemed pretty pissed and said he would talk to you himself. Otherwise, he didn't fuck with us."

"I'll go by his house in a little while. Right now, it's time to get started for real." I reached down and picked up the bag I'd left with Lucille. "There's two birds in here. We're gonna cook them up and break them down. After I deal with Fred, I want you to get with the kids here on Bethune, Greenhurst, Bunche, and Ezzard Charles. Put them all down. Just bring Boar or Vic back a thousand on each ounce. I'll square each of you up on Fridays. Cool?"

Everybody nodded.

"I'm going to show you all how I want the shit cooked and cut up when I get back. For now, we'll do it here. We're going to need a place just to cook and cut the dope soon. Be thinking about it. Come on, Slick. We'll be back."

My cousin and I walked out and got in my truck.

"How did it go at the Medical Center?"

"All right. I got the info we need."

"We'll work on that later. Just me, you, Jas, and maybe Boar Hog are gonna handle the chemical shit. Stay at Boar's house for a while until we get everything set up. We going to see a nigger now about these streets over here. I don't really expect too much trouble, but be ready."

We drove the couple of blocks to Cathcart and stopped in front of a two-story brick house near the corner. From here I could see the spot where Herman and his boys had shot at me. Parkes Street and Miss Jennings's house were just across Little York. Fred Jackson's Navigator was parked in the driveway.

We got out and walked up to the front door. My knock was immediately followed by a gruff, questioning voice.

"Who is it?"

"Chris King."

After a moment, the front door opened. A tall, slim black man in his mid-twenties stood there.

"What's up, Moochie? Fred around?" Moochie was Fred's cousin. They were always together.

"Who's this?"

"My cousin, Vic. Cuz, this is Moochie Jackson. We'll probably be doing business together."

This threw Moochie, like I figured it would, and he dropped some of the attitude. I knew Fred's woman and children stayed here, so I figured if there was any drama, it wouldn't go down here.

"Come on in. Fred's in the back."

We followed him through the house, which was reasonably clean and well furnished for a crib with three little rug rats running around.

Fred sat in an easy chair in the den, which looked out on the patio. "Lil' King, what's up? I hear you been doin' big things."

Fred Jackson used to be one of my old man's lieutenants and had run the very streets I'd just told the Colliers to supply. When Big George got arrested, Fred had simply branched out on his own. I had no problem with that, except that, as far as I was concerned, I had more right to sell dope there than anyone.

"Not yet. I intend to, though. I heard you had a talk with Frank Collier."

"Yeah, he was slinging somebody else's dope on my street."

"Well, Fred, that's a matter of opinion. That's why I

came to see you. If Bethune belongs to anybody, which I happen to think it don't, I figure it belongs to me. Big George had that whole area sewed up. You know this. Hell, you used to work for him. I'm his son, my dope comes from his connect, and I got his blessing. Am I missing something here?"

Fred's light-skinned face got red. "Damn right, you missing something! You missing the fact that your old man been gone a while. Things have changed."

"Fred, I'll be straight up with you. My daddy said that you was a real reasonable, straight-up dude. You never came short, and you always handled your business. He got much respect for you. That's the only reason we having this conversation. A little while back, some niggers told me I couldn't sling in one of my daddy's old spots. They probably regretted it."

Moochie stepped forward. "You little—"

Fred, his eyes locked with mine, said to his cousin, "Chill, Mooch, I got this."

Vic's hand came from under his shirt when Moochie backed off.

"Look, Fred, I didn't come by here to piss on you. I came by, as a show of respect to my father's wishes, to give you some news, and to make you an offer. The news is, I'm gonna take over where my daddy left off, then I'm gonna build on that. That's real. The offer is this—If you want to score the best dope, like what King George used to sell, I'll give you a good price. You don't have to work for me, though you would probably end up making more money than what you're making now.

You really don't want to work against me. This is my cousin. Any deal you make with him, you make with me. Any disrespect you show him, you show me."

Fred sat silent for what seemed like a whole minute.

"How old are you, Chris? Nineteen, twenty?"

" 'Bout that."

"You really think you can take and hold George's territory? Some pretty tough niggers done grabbed some of it."

"I know I can, and I will."

"What you offering me?"

"I'm offering Bunche, Ezzard Charles, and Bland. Ounces for seven hundred. If you want to buy weight, I'll cut you a deal, but it won't be the same dope."

"Your shit as good as George's was?"

"Or better. If you want to check it out, go to Frank Collier and tell him I said give you a half-ounce. All the smokers gonna want this shit. Word."

"And all the youngsters slinging still work for me?"

"Except for the Colliers, yeah. If they sling on Bethune, McWilliams, Greenhurst, or Covington, though, they score from me. You do too. My people won't fuck with yours, and vice versa. You the only one in the hood getting this offer."

"What about the others?"

I let my face get hard. "They get what I give them, or they get to talk to Herman."

"Understand something, youngster. I'm gonna take you up on your offer for two reasons. One, it's good business. I know personally that your daddy's dope gonna outsell all the rest. Two, I got much respect for George. You his son, so I got to respect that too. Don't get it twisted, though. I don't fear no nigger."

"Don't *you* get it twisted, Fred. I don't want you or anybody else to fear me. Them niggers stepped to me. Anybody leave me alone and let me handle mine won't have no problem from me. I'm glad we're going to work together. We'll both make money, and I always try to follow my daddy's advice."

"Well, you got yourself a deal, Chris. Let's drink on it."

While Moochie poured up some Hennessy, Vic and I gave Fred our digits. I told him to look for my cousin at Boar Hog's until he got his own place.

As we drove away later, I was satisfied.

I wasn't fooled, though. None of the other spots would be as easy as this one to lock down.

Chapter Seventeen

As we left Fred Jackson's house, my mind was working furiously. I was overjoyed that things with Fred had gone so well. At the same time, I knew that my moves had to be done with the utmost care and planning. Fred was definitely right about one thing—None of the rest of the spots would be easy.

"Say, cuz, tell me about the Medical Center."

"Things are still the same. The shipment from Costa will come in two weeks from Thursday. It gets there just after nine in the morning. I double-checked the logs, and the same driver has been doing the route for the past year. Charlie Logan, big, country dude. Likes to talk a lot about how much pussy he gets."

We sat in front of Boar Hog's house while I thought it over. A plan had started to form, but I didn't like it too much. It involved Jas, and while I knew she was down, and would do whatever I asked, I didn't want to ask this.

"How can we find out where he lives?"

"I already thought of that. I'll just have to follow him for a day or two. Unless you got a better idea, we'll just have to jack him for the shit somewhere along his route."

"I'm working on an idea. Go on and find out all you can about him and let me know. Boar can handle shit here for a couple of days. Look, we've got enough shit to really come up. Sixty birds will net us over a couple mil, selling stone for stone. What's really good is that it's ours. We don't owe anybody for it. I never thought I would say this, but that's chump change. And it only works if the shit is primo. What we're gonna do is work the ten birds from José while we wait on the lick to amp up the other shit.

"I got a hundred things to try and keep straight, and I'm gonna need you to help. Nobody's gonna give us what we want. We gotta take it. And we're gonna take it all."

"Why we sittin' here talkin' then? Let's do it."

We went inside, and I laid out the deal I made with Fred. I sent the Colliers out to choose and organize the youngsters who were gonna work our streets. I had given Fred Bland Street, which was a pretty good location with a lot of dopeheads. From Cathcart to Wheatly was a straight shot about a quarter-mile down the street, and the law rarely came through.

I was counting on the Jacksons working for me,

whether they realized it or not. Bethune, where we were, was one of the best spots in this part of the hood. With what we were paying, I knew the Colliers could pick and choose who would sling our rocks.

We all went into the kitchen, and while I cooked the dope, I explained how we would handle this. All the money would come to Vic or Boar Hog, and Vic would be responsible for the split.

"Thirty-four gees comes to me or Jas from these two. When you run out of fingers and toes, get a damn calculator, cuz."

"Fuck you. I can count better than you any day of the week. You just keep the shit coming."

"Okay, smart ass. What's everybody else's cut?"

He thought a minute. "I get thirteen. Frank, Freddie, and Boar each get seven."

"Damn! Okay, you win. Nigger did learn something in school, besides how to smoke weed and cut class. When the first ten are gone, we need to set up a house to keep the shit. I wanna be ready by the time the word really gets out there."

My phone rang. Jas told me that she and Mama had finished their business. She asked me to meet her at her mother's house in forty-five minutes. After I hung up, I told Boar and Vic I'd holler at them later.

When I got to the corner, instead of taking the right that led toward Jas' moms, I went left. I cruised across Carver Road and pulled into the parking lot at the corner of Easter and Little York. On the side where I parked was a liquor store, a convenience store, and a barbecue joint. Across Easter Street was a car wash and another convenience store.

This place, called The Corner by residents of Acres Home, was one of the hottest dope spots, if not the hottest, in Houston. Young men stood together in groups, and the traffic was continuous. Cars rolled up from all four directions. Kids on both sides of Easter would run up to the vehicles and serve their product. These boys didn't care who they served.

The cops all knew about the spot. Every now and then they would make a half-hearted raid, but it was a waste of time. Like killing roaches in a hovel.

When the yell, "Five *O*!" went up, the youngsters would scatter in every direction. With the number of stabbings and shootings that occurred daily around here, no cop in his right mind would chase them on foot.

I sat and watched the action for a minute. A couple of the young slingers started my way, but turned around when they saw who it was.

Finally I saw Trey Deuce. Trey was a sixteen-year-old basketball wizard who could hit almost at will from anywhere on the court. Six-two and skinny as a rail, in a better world his future would've been already secure, but an abusive alcoholic father and a crackhead mother were too much to overcome. He found his acceptance on the streets, and the basketball court at Carver Park, a few blocks away.

Nickel-and-dime hustling here at The Corner, neutral

territory, was how he kept his three little sisters and two brothers fed. Mama and Daddy sure weren't gonna do it. A proud, angry kid, he refused to work with a crew. I liked Trey. The boy had heart.

I tapped my horn and waved him over.

"*C*! What's the word? When we gonna ball?"

"Yo, Trey. It's all good. Get in a minute and take a ride with me."

As we headed west, toward T. C. Jester, I told him, "Yo, check this out. I want to run a business proposal by you. I know you out here hustling for yours. I'm gonna make a couple of moves myself. You want some work?"

"You gonna front me? I ain't got enough to cop. You know I'm good for it."

I knew that damn near every dime he hustled went to his people. Every day he came to The Corner, he started with ten or twenty dollars, and shaved and flipped until he came up on seventy-five to a hundred dollars.

"Tell you what. I'll give you fifty stones. Real bricks. You bring me back a grand. That leaves a grand for you if you split them. I'll keep the front up for a week. After that, you buy your own."

It was a sweetheart deal. Instead of splitting the rocks to make two twenties each, he would probably make at least sixty dollars a stone. The people who scored on The Corner were not from the hood. In fact a lot of them were white. You could come up quick slinging there, if you could handle the drama.

Like I figured, he jumped on the deal.

"Now, I ain't dealing with no one else who usually works The Corner. This shit is the bomb, an' if anybody else up there wants it, they gotta go through you. Here." I peeled off two hundred dollars from my roll and handed it over.

He took it, a questioning expression on his face.

"Go over to Boar Hog's house on Bethune. Tell him I said to give you an *O-Z*. When you work it, take him or my cousin the money. You'll see my nigga there when you talk to Boar. This is just between you an' me. Take that money and do something for your people."

"Why you doin' this for me, man?"

" 'Cause you good people, and 'cause you got a mean jumpshot." I smiled at him. "Just be careful and do the right thing."

"Yo, dawg, you ain't got to worry about that. Thanks."

On our ride, I had made a big circle, and was already thinking about how to make a play on some of the spots we had passed. I dropped him off at the corner of Little York and Bethune and went to meet Jas.

Chapter Eighteen

Jas' mother lived near the corner of Dolly Wright and Parkes. Parkes was a short street that dead-ended into a narrow strip of pine woods, and picked up and ran to Little York, directly across from The Alley, where all this had started only a few weeks ago. The little wood-framed house needed work. The paint was peeling, and the front porch sagged. Jas' mother worked as an assistant manager for Sears down on Shepherd, a couple of miles from Acres Home. A little on the plump side, she was in her forties, and was a looker. And when she stood in the same room with her daughters, you knew where they got their looks.

When I pulled into the yard, Jasmine came to the door with a huge smile. I knew her business had gone well. I was struck by her beauty. In no time at all, she had become an intricate part of my life. I was a lucky man.

"Hey, baby!" She ran down the steps and threw herself into my arms.

I hugged her. Over her shoulder, I noticed a couple of faces in the doorway.

She pulled me by the hand into the front room.

As my eyes adjusted to the gloom, I heard a voice.

"Well, well, if it ain't the young man who done stole my child." Jasmine's mother came out of the kitchen, drying her hands on a dishcloth.

"Hey, Miss Sharon. An' right now, I don't know who stole who."

"Well, I do."

I turned to the new voice. No matter how many times I looked at her, I couldn't help but wonder how much Chenise looked like Jas. Three years older, she already had two children by two different men. Chenise wore her hair short, and her breasts weren't quite as big as Jasmine's, but in almost every other aspect, they were identical. The same paper bag complexion, the same light brown eyes, and that same world-class ass.

I had always fantasized about fucking her ever since puberty, as well as half the men in the hood. The other half probably did, because she was wild. Her oldest was seven. She was fifteen when she had him. Her three-year-old baby girl clung to her thighs now.

"Then tell me."

"Jas has been after your fine little ass since elementary. That's the only reason I didn't rape your young butt myself."

"Nisey, don't start no shit," Jas said.

"See what I mean? The little bitch is serious too. I damn sure don't wanna fight her bad ass, so I guess you safe." Chenise laughed.

I still felt there was something that I didn't quite get.

"*Q*, Shayla, go thank your Uncle Chris for the stuff he and Aunt Jas bought for you."

Quinton came barreling from the back. "Thanks, Chris. That Xbox and the games are phat! You come up, huh. Y'all getting married or what?"

"Boy, get your little ass back in that room an' stay out of grown folks' business. Sit down, baby, an' don't pay any attention to these fools. You got the only sane one in the whole bunch." A look of complete sadness came over Miss Sharon's face as she looked over my shoulder.

"Hey, Chris!"

It was Yolanda, Jas' baby sister. Only fifteen, she was beautiful in her own right. Darker than her sisters, she was a little fuller in the body, but her true beauty was her eyes. Such innocence and trust was seldom seen these days. Yolanda was slightly retarded.

"Yo-Yo, come give me a hug. You been a good girl?"

"Yes! Jas says you gonna buy me some toys!"

As I hugged her, I looked over at Jasmine and smiled. "Then that's just what we're gonna do."

"When?"

I looked over at Jas again.

"Baby, the lawyer's office was out I-10. Your mama and me stopped at Memorial City Mall, and I got the game for *Q*. I promised I'd take her to Northline later. You wanna come?"

"Sure."

Yolanda had always been one of my favorite people. Whenever I saw her, I gave her money for sweets. I didn't mind spoiling her at all.

A strange feeling was coming over me. I was just beginning to realize what being with Jasmine really meant. I can't say I wasn't a little scared.

After a delicious soul food meal, Jas, her two sisters, and I piled into the car and headed out to the mall, while Miss Sharon stayed with *Q*.

The afternoon was fun. Yolanda went crazy in the toy store. Jas and Chenise kept trying to make her put stuff back, but I overruled them every time. She ended up getting almost five hundred dollars in toys, and Jas and Chenise bought a ton of clothes.

I was getting off on the looks I was getting from the men. These sisters were hot. Whenever we passed some sister who checked me out, Jas and Chenise would lean in and caress me and roll their eyes. I again remarked to myself how much they looked like twins, an idea that didn't take full effect until the next morning.

We stayed at Miss Sharon's so late, drinking Hennessy and talking, that she insisted we spend the night. I was in no shape to argue, so I called Vic and told him where I was. Jas and I slept in her old bed.

* * *

The next morning, I woke up hungover and hungry. I put on the robe Jas had bought, and stumbled to the bathroom. Then I went looking for my girl. I found her in the kitchen. Her back to me, she had on a short housecoat, and a scarf around her hair. She was cracking eggs into a bowl. That fabulous ass was looking good as she moved back and forth.

She hadn't noticed me in the doorway, so I eased up behind her. My dick got hard as a brick as I stepped into that ass and reached around for a double handful of tits. "We can eat at home. I want to do you. Now."

She reached behind her without turning around and grabbed my dick. It was just about that time that I noticed something was wrong. Jasmine's breasts were big, with thick, long nipples, but these breasts were smaller, and the nipples were small, hard lumps as I pinched them.

"I don't think Jas would like that, but for all this, I just might take a chance." Chenise turned around, letting my dick go, and laughed her ass off at me standing there, dick sticking out from between my robe, mouth wide open with shock.

I felt like an idiot. The really bad thing was that, right then, I wanted nothing more than to bend her over and stick my rod in her.

I finally got myself under control. Stuffing my dick back in, I muttered, "One of you ought to wear a bell."

Chenise was looking at me with a mixture of amusement and desire. I suppose my face reflected the same thing, except for the amusement part.

"I'm sorry, baby. I thought you were—"

"Jasmine. I know. You ain't the first. None of the others tried to stick their dick in me, though. Too bad she's my sister."

"Where is she?"

"She had to go get your mom for something. She told me to tell you to call her. What's it worth to you for me not to tell her you just tried to fuck me?"

"About the same thing it's worth for me not to tell her you tried to wring my dick off."

"Get out of here, boy. Go get dressed. Breakfast will be ready in a minute."

I beat feet.

While I was pulling my pants on, it hit me. Chenise would be perfect for setting up Logan. If her fine ass could make me want to risk all I had with Jas, imagine what she could do to a pussy hound like Logan.

I finished dressing and hurried back to the kitchen. "Say, sis, how would you like to make ten thousand dollars?"

"Don't play with me, Chris. Who I gotta kill?"

"Nobody. I just need you to set this dude up for me."

"Set him up? I ain't getting involved in no murder. I got babies."

"Not that way. We're just gonna rob his truck. All you got to do is get his nose open so he won't know what's up."

"I got to fuck him?"

"Maybe."

"You know I ain't no ho. For ten gees, though, I'd fuck the whole Houston Rockets team. I'll do it."

"Good. Let me make sure Jas is okay with it."

"My little sis don't run my life."

"No, but I got to live with her."

"Boy, you couldn't run her off with a stick. Talk to her then."

Though Chenise's words about me and Jas made me feel good, she couldn't have been more wrong.

Chapter Nineteen

Two days later, I sat in Boar Hog's bedroom with the Colliers, Vic, and Boar. We were discussing how fast the dope was selling.

"At this rate, youngster, we gon' be out by the weekend. You need to get some more ready."

"All right, Boar. What's the deal on that house we talked about? The one over on Greenhurst?"

Frank Collier spoke up. "The plumbing leaks, as well as the roof. I can get it for about five thousand in back taxes. Want me to go ahead?"

"Yeah. There is too much traffic around here. Do what you got to. Keep track of what you got to spend, and Vic will pay you back. Put in metal doors and burglar bars. We'll work out of there."

"Okay. I'll try to have it ready by next week."

The house would only be a temporary measure. We

needed to get a place in the hood that was pretty much jack-proof.

Things were taking off like they had a life of their own. Vic had found out that Charlie Logan lived in an apartment complex in Greenspoint, and that the company he worked for, Costa, had its main offices and warehouse out near Intercontinental Airport.

Charlie had the same routine every morning. He'd be at Costa at six to load his truck and get his delivery tickets. Then he'd stop at the Waffle House near the freeway to have breakfast before heading south on his route.

Jas was okay with using Chenise to trap Logan. I think she appreciated the fact that I didn't want her to do it. I took a ribbing for mistaking her sister for her, but Chenise must have cleaned up what happened, because she didn't seem too upset.

Vic and Chenise had really hit it off. I think they were both attracted by their similar natures. Tomorrow, I was going to take Chenise to the Waffle House and try and put her on to Logan. Vic couldn't do it because he already knew him. The way things looked, we were going to need that pharmaceutical coke soon.

I left and drove to Bear Creek. I had barely opened the door when Jasmine jumped me.

"We got it! Baby, it's ours!"

"What?" I asked, holding on to her.

"The shop! Your momma's so happy. Me too." With that she kissed me.

One thing led to another, and soon I was weak-kneed as she sucked my dick, her soft hands gently cupping my balls. Somehow we both got naked without her missing one beat.

When I couldn't take it anymore, I pushed her to her knees and entered her hot, dripping pussy. I just couldn't get enough of Jasmine. Her beautiful ass pushing back against me, and her soft moans of ecstasy pushed me over the edge.

After I spurted into her, crying out her name, we lay spent on the living room floor.

"Chris?"

"Yeah, baby?"

"You won't get mad if I ask you something?"

"No, I won't get mad."

"Do you love me?"

I had been wrestling with that same question for weeks. When she asked, the answer was suddenly obvious to me. "Yes, baby, you know I do."

"Well, I prayed you did. I didn't know for sure. You know I love you, that I'd do anything for you, don't you?"

"I guess I do."

"Anything except one. I won't share you. I don't want anybody but you. I never did. But you're a man. I know how so many of them are. Just tell me if you find somebody you want more than me. Will you do that?"

"Jas, how in the world could I ever want anybody but you? You got it all, ma."

"Just promise."

"Okay. If I ever meet a hoochie I want more than you, I'll tell you. Happy?"

"Very." She started to suck on my neck.

I was suddenly overcome with feeling for her. She was the one. I knew one way to really let her know. "Jas, let's—"

"Sssh." She put her fingers over my mouth. "Not yet. That's not what I was after. It's enough to know that I'm yours and you're mine. We still got work to do."

I stood, picked her up, and carried her to our bed. Throughout the long, sweet afternoon of lovemaking, I vowed to never let anything come between us.

The next morning, I picked Chenise up at 5:30. We drove to the Waffle House and ordered breakfast. We sat near the front.

At 7:30, a big brown truck pulled in. A fat, tall black man got out and came into the restaurant. As he passed our table, I winked at Chenise.

From the corner of my eye, I noticed the dude gawking at her. Who wouldn't? She had on tight silk pants with matching blouse, and her hair and makeup were perfect. Shit, she looked damn good to me, and I slept with her image every night.

At my nod, she got up and walked to the restroom. I thought Logan was gonna have a heart attack. That ass was bangin'!

I got up and walked outside to the car. Sitting in the

driver's seat, I saw Chenise come from the restroom area and pause next to Logan's table. She looked around anxiously before bending to ask him a question. I knew she was asking if he'd seen where her brother had disappeared to. I could see that Logan was hooked.

I sat a few minutes while Chenise chatted him up. When he patted his pockets for a pen, I started back in.

"Sean! Sean! Come here. I want you to meet my new friend. When you ran off, I thought I was going to have to get a ride home."

She had played it perfectly. I went and met Logan. We talked about casual bullshit, while Chenise made eyes at him. I went to pay while she made him promise to call at a certain time, to avoid a jealous boyfriend, and we left.

As we drove off, I smiled at her. "Perfect, baby. He'll have a hard dick all day."

"When he calls, I'll tell him how hot he made me. Pity that we can only meet early in the morning because of my no-good boyfriend. I'll have him at the Greenspoint Inn first thing tomorrow morning. Then I'll keep him panting until you're ready."

"I couldn't have done this without you."

"Yes, you could. Tell the truth—You just didn't want Jas to do it. You know I'm going to have to fuck him tomorrow to seal the deal."

What could I say? She was right. Rather than let Jas sleep with that fat pig, I would have just straight jacked the truck, which would have been much riskier.

"Look, sis, if you don't—"

Chenise held up her hand. "Naw, it ain't that. You told me the deal from the git-go. Lord knows I gave away enough free pussy that I'd be a fool not to do this and get paid. It's just that, you know, me and your cousin been spending a lot of time together. I don't want him to think . . . you know."

"Listen, Chenise, Vic's my boy. We're more like brothers than cousins. Believe me, you got nothin' to worry about. He thinks you're a superstar for being down with helping us like this. Know what else he said?"

"What?"

"He said that if that fat fucker looked at you wrong, he would fuck him up. How you do what you do is up to you. Anything Vic wants to know he's gotta find out from you. Long as you ain't fucking over him, I'm out of it."

She sat in silence for a while. "Thanks, Chris."

"No problem. I'll tell you one more thing. You look so good, and your shit is so much together, if I wasn't stone in love with Jas, I'd give cuz a run for his money. And that's word."

Her smile lit up the car. She leaned over and kissed me on the cheek. "I guess sis better not fuck up, then, huh?"

Chapter Twenty

It was two weeks later. The next morning we were due to hit Logan's truck. I only had three birds of the dope I'd gotten from José left. Business was so good, I didn't want to expand our territory until I had more supply. Me, Boar Hog, and Vic were counting money in Boar Hog's room.

"Word is getting around that you taking your daddy's place and coming up with the best dope. I ain't telling you your business, but maybe you ought to keep a lower profile."

"Boar, I can't right now. There's too much to do."

"Then figure out a way to do it without you being on front street. Yo' daddy still fighting his case, so them feds would like no more than to bust his son and add that to his charges, not to mention sending you away."

"He's right, cuz. It's one thing for niggers to know you

running the show. It's another for them to prove it. We need a line into the substation."

He was talking about the police substation up on West Montgomery near Garden City. I was already working on that.

Mama and Jas had opened their new business, called Hair & More. We were just starting to shoot money through there. If the cops got onto me now, it would fuck everything up.

"All right, I hear you. It's more risk, but from now on, you two do all the collecting and bring the money to Mama or Jas at the salon until we get a better place. Don't forget to pay the rent on Mayview for Trey. After tomorrow, I'll have enough keys to hold us awhile. Then we move on Garapan, Druid, and Nuben."

Trey Deuce had been slinging so much shit on The Corner that I had rented him a house a few blocks away over on Mayview. I was in the process of getting it fortified so I could store dope there. Trey had assembled a crew of five teenage killers. The boy had done well.

Just then the night was filled with noise. Gunshots.

"What the fuck?"

Boar was already on his knees, reaching under the bed, and Vic's cell went off.

"Greenhurst!" Boar yelled.

I grabbed the AR-15, and Boar and Vic each got shotguns. We were always packing our pistols. We ran out the front door to Greenhurst, two streets over from Bethune. Both streets dead-ended at a stand of woods riddled with walking paths, and a couple of the paths went clear through to Wilburforce, about forty yards beyond the dead end.

We didn't take the cars. I motioned Boar Hog toward the path at the end of Bethune. That would bring him up on the south side of our dope house, nearest the woods. Vic followed me through the yards. We only had to jump one fence to be in somebody's backyard on McWilliams, and one more fence and we'd be on Greenhurst. I chose the yards that would bring us out two houses north of ours.

There were two SUV's parked in the yard of the dope house, where four men were blasting away at the door and windows. The metal doors and frames I had told Frank to get were holding up. For now.

I sent Vic and his shotgun toward the rear. I stepped out, and with the selector switch on auto, opened up at the men with three-shot bursts. Two of them went down. The other two turned toward where I was half-concealed by some hedges and cut loose at me. Shit. One of them had an AK. I was fucked.

Just then, I heard the sweetest sound in the world—two 12-gauge shotguns letting loose multiple rounds. I raised my head to see that the four men were all down. Vic stood on the porch waving me on. I trotted over. The smell was awful.

One of the would-be jackers had his face blown completely off. Another had been ripped apart in the middle by the buckshot. By contrast, the two that I'd hit looked pretty good. They were just as dead, though.

Boar Hog yelled for the Colliers to open the doors.

Frank pulled the bullet-riddled door open, his face tight with anger.

I asked, "Anybody hit?"

"Fred got cut by glass from the window. It's not too bad."

"Let's clean out of here quick."

Me, Frank, Fred, Vic, Boar, and the two workers grabbed all the dope and money. I tried to wipe as many surfaces as I could, while we had time. One of Frank's runners whistled. We knew the cops were almost here, so we all headed for the woods.

"Where to?" Fred panted.

"Back to Boar Hog's. The cops know about the paths. They might be on Wilburforce."

We ran all the way back to Boar's.

While Lucille bandaged Fred's neck and arm, we had a meeting.

"Who the fuck were those niggers?"

"I ain't sure, Chris, but I think they're from Greenspoint. I'll find out, though."

Fuck! The Greenspoint Posse was notorious. If this was them, then we had a real beef on our hands. I wasn't sure we were strong enough yet to take them on. I didn't consider myself to be a real gangsta, but I was a man. If you fucked with me or mine, you better be ready. Ask Herman.

"Find out all you can. Don't worry. We'll get ours. Right now, shut everything down around here for a few days. Have a couple of your boys work Covington up by the hamburger stand. Tell our customers we'll be back in business in a couple of days."

Vic said, "That's it for tonight. Everybody go home. Give me all the money."

Soon there was nobody in the room but me, Boar, and Vic. We cleaned the guns and were putting them away, when we heard a scuffle at the back door, and the door slam.

Lucille drug a young girl in by the hair. The girl was screaming and fighting, and Lucille was cuffing her and cussing while she forced her into the room. "Bitch! No-good snitchin' ho, you gonna tell them what you know."

Lucille stopped before me. She had been true to her word. She had cleaned up and put on a few pounds. She looked pretty good. And she stuck to Boar Hog like glue.

"Chris, this bitch from Greenspoint. She used to hang and get high with us. When we quit giving her dope, she got pissed. Carolyn told me she said she was gonna sic her uncles from Greenspoint on us."

"When Fred said he thought they were from Greenspoint, I went and found this ho." Lucille slapped the girl again. "Now tell him, 'fore I get my knife."

Trembling, the girl started, "I'm sorry. They said they was jus' gonna take the dope an' money, an' nobody was gonna get hurt. I'm sorry."

I walked closer to her. "Who said?"

"My Uncle Johnny an' his brothers. I'm sorry."

I walked past the sobbing girl and motioned to Lucille to follow me into the kitchen. “Thanks, baby. You probably saved us a lot of trouble.”

“Don’t worry about it. And don’t worry about her. I’ll handle that.”

Looking into Lucille’s eyes, I realized that there was a depth to her that I’d never imagined. I leaned down and kissed her on the cheek. “See you later, baby.”

She smiled, knowing that I had fully accepted her at last.

When Lucille had taken the girl out, Boar Hog spoke up. “Why don’t you two go on home? I know the nigger that runs Greenspoint. I’m-a call him and talk. I don’t think those assholes were working for anybody but themselves. If there’s a problem, I’ll call you. Y’all got important work to do in the morning.”

We left. The night’s events served as a wake-up call for me. To go to the top of this game, I’d have to stay on top of my game.

Chapter Twenty-one

We sat in the back of the Waffle House waiting for a call from Chenise. A few miles down I-45 South was the Greenspoint Inn, a popular local motel. For the last two weeks, Chenise had met Logan there, and they started what he believed was an intense affair. The dude was sprung.

According to Chenise, she'd only given him some pussy once, the day after we'd seen him in this same joint. She said that she put that monkey on him so good, he was actually in tears, and since that morning, he'd literally been begging for her to go to the motel with him again. She had held out, making excuses that her old man was watching her. On the couple of occasions when she gave him a blowjob in his truck, to keep him on the hook, she promised to work out a way they could really be together, so he was primed and ready.

Yesterday, before dropping her off and going over to Boar Hog's, me and Vic went to the Greenspoint Inn and rented a room upstairs, on the back side, for two days.

My cell rang.

"Chris?"

"Yeah, ma."

"We'll be leaving here in a few. The chump don't even want to wait till I finish my coffee."

"We'll be there."

I looked over at Vic. "It's time."

I pulled out, drove under the freeway, and took 45 South.

At the motel, I pulled around the main building and parked at the rear of the back parking lot. We got out and let ourselves into the room with my key. We laid our masks and pistols on the bed and proceeded to wipe down the room. As far as I knew, neither our prints nor Chenise's were on record, but with the shit the laws had these days, better safe than sorry.

When Vic signaled from his position by the window that Logan's truck was rounding the building, we pulled on the masks and stepped into the bathroom.

A minute or so later, the room door opened.

"Oh, baby, I been waiting for this." Logan was literally panting.

"Hold on, baby. I know we don't have much time. You got to go to work, and I got to go pacify that nigger. Take your clothes off and get ready while I go pee."

The bathroom door eased open. The look on Logan's

face when we stepped out into the room was priceless. Sitting on the side of the bed with his dick in his hand, his mouth fell open, and his eyes actually crossed. The boy looked like a scared rabbit.

"Freeze, nigger!" My yell was kind of overkill.

Vic walked over to the bed and bitch-slapped him.

I put my hand on his arm to hold him back. That wasn't in the script. I wondered if Logan wasn't the only one that thang of Chenise's had sprung lately.

"Just do like we say, and you won't be hurt. We didn't come here for a homicide, but it's your choice."

The dude started to blabber. "Don't shoot me! You can take anything you want. Just let me go!"

I looked over at Vic and shrugged. Vic's move, though not part of the plan, may have been the right one. The nigger was straight bitch. We had him pinned, sure, but at least he could have been a real man about it.

"Chill." I picked up Logan's pants and made a show of going through his pockets. I took his wallet and keys.

He wasn't even looking at me. He was watching Vic. When Chenise walked back into the room, he started with, "Why you—"

That was as far as he got. Vic clocked him upside his head with his pistol this time.

Whimpering, Logan fell back on the bed, hands held to his bleeding head

"On your face. Now!" I was fed up with this dude. We weren't really rushed. This time of the morning, the only people really moving around the motel were the crack-heads, but I just wanted to do the damn thing and split.

I removed the plastic ties from my pocket, strapped Logan's hands and feet together, and gagged him with the cloth I'd brought for that purpose.

Since the room had been rented without ID, and we weren't around enough for somebody to really remember, there was no way to connect Logan to us when he was found. I think my cousin would have been okay with cappin' him.

I slid the truck's rear door up and looked in. *Damn!* The pharmaceutical business must have been booming. The shelves built into the sides, as well as most of the floor space, were filled with boxes of drugs. It took a few minutes for Vic to locate the cases with the cocaine, marked poison.

There were three boxes with four containers each. They were heavy, and it took about fifteen minutes to transfer them to our SUV. When we were done, Vic jumped back into Logan's truck.

When I asked what was in the small box he took, he answered, "Demerol."

Originally, I had planned to lock the truck and just fade away with what we needed. As Vic jumped to the ground with the package of Demerol, I got a better idea. Why not just leave the door open and up. In this hood, it would take no time for the word to get out that there was a truck full of prescription drugs sitting wide open at the Greenspoint Inn. That would surely screw up any investigation into the jacking.

I looked over my shoulder at Chenise. She was still holding down the parking lot. I was tempted to locate some "syrup" while we were there, but common sense said it was time to split, so we did.

We drove to Bear Creek. Chenise became the third person, the others being Jas and me, to know the location of the condo. After lugging the boxes upstairs, I took the small box Vic had grabbed and read the label while him and Chenise were squeezing up on each other.

I discovered that Demerol was the brand name for the drug meperidine, a synthetic narcotic for pain. Was my boy crazy? We went to get pure, uncut pharmaceutical coke, and he grabs synthetic heroin?

I hated to break up the Hallmark moment, but I wanted some answers. Now. "Say, Slick?"

Vic broke his liplock with Chenise without letting her go. "That shit is probably the most popular painkiller in hospitals, cuz. It's not as addictive as morphine or heroin, and it works instantly. After last night, I figured we might just need to keep some around. It ain't for sale."

His words had a real sobering effect on me. He was right. "Good lookin' out, cuz. Now before you and sis get to swapping spit again, come help me with this shit."

We opened a case. Just like Vic had described it, the cocaine hydrochloride came in five-pound containers inscribed with skull and crossbones and the warning that the contents were deadly. I lifted one of the jars and cut it open. The crystalline product looked just like the good shit I'd gotten from José, except there were no lumps.

"Don't let the looks fool you. That shit is hot. One of the residents at Herman a few years ago decided that he could use some of this shit to help him stay alert on the double-shifts they were always making them work. Since he had friends who did coke, he thought he knew better than the textbooks. The shot he took busted his heart. It was hushed up, as far as the public was concerned, but the people who worked there knew the real deal."

"Shit. I think we have to play with it until we can figure out how much to cut each bird with. We want some good shit, but it ain't good business to kill off all your customers. We're going to need each batch tested."

Chenise said, "That means you're gonna have to work on it in the hood. Why don't you do it at my Aunt Clara's house? That way, you can have all the testers you want right across the street."

I looked over at her. "Girl, you a genius. I might need to give you a job. Wait here a minute."

I went into the bedroom and returned with two stacks of money, which I gave to her. "Here's twenty for the job you did."

"But—"

"I know we agreed on ten, but I think you deserve a bonus. Jas does too, 'cause she's the one who left it out for you."

"I think you deserve one too. I'll give you mine later." Vic palmed her ass, and they were mooning at each other again.

I wondered if me and Jasmine looked so weird when

we were together. We probably did. I just hoped Vic knew what he was doing.

"Let's get going. Vic, weigh out a half-pound of that shit. I'll get a half-ki' of that fucked-up shit, an' we'll go try and hook this shit up."

Twenty minutes later, we were on our way to Acres Home.

Chapter Twenty-two

On the long ride to The Four-Four, I figured out how I was going to do this. We stopped at Wal-Mart and bought a few Pyrex measuring cups and some baking soda. These and some digital scales were the only equipment we would need.

After sending Chenise up to the beauty shop to see Jas, Vic and me went to work. First, I rocked up an eight ball (one-eighth ounce of cocaine) of the shit we'd stolen from the Mexicans. I put that aside, weighed out an ounce, added a sixteenth of the synthetic, and cooked it up.

Next I added an eighth of pure to an ounce. Then a quarter. I kept the cooked dope carefully segregated.

I saw one problem already. First things first, though, I wanted the ratio right.

Vic left to go get the testers. I should have known better, because he came back with three females and one male. One of the females was Carolyn. Since Lucille stopped smoking, Carolyn and some of the girls that used to hang at Boar Hog's started hanging in The Alley, where one of them, Myra, lived.

Miss Jennings's kitchen was crowded, but I didn't want these crackheads running loose in the house. Plus, I wanted to watch the reactions as they hit each batch of dope. Like all dedicated "rockhounds," they all had their own tools.

"I got four different kinds of dope I want you to try. I want to know which one is the best. Be for real. Don't get greedy and try to load up your pipes for later. Don't try to palm any. Do this for me, and I'll take care of you real good. Deal?"

They nodded their heads simultaneously, like they'd rehearsed it.

I gave them each a hit of the first rock. The one I hadn't cut.

"This shit is weak," Carolyn said to Vic. "Ain't nearly as good as what you got on Bethune."

Myra and the others agreed.

I had them clean their pipes and put in new screens. They didn't bitch much because they would have a screen full of dope stashed from each batch they tested. I was giving them major hits.

I could see when Myra blew out a huge cloud of smoke from the batch I'd cut with a sixteenth that this was more potent.

When Carolyn was done and could talk again, she verified my thoughts. "This is much better. Maybe not quite as good as the Bethune shit, but good enough to sell."

Once again they cleaned and reloaded their pipes.

I opened the front and back doors and let some of the smoke out. The major reason the crack habit is so expensive is that that first big hit, the one that blows your mind and makes you hear bells, is the only real one you're gonna get. The rest of the time, you're spending vast amounts of money chasing something you can't catch.

I figured that if this batch had given them a real good hit then the dope would have to be a lot better in order for them to catch a really good buzz off the next hit. I was right. The batch I had added an eighth to hit them even harder than the last one. Instead of their third major hit in thirty minutes, the testers were rocked like it was their first in months.

"Shit, man. That's the one! My pussy just flooded, and my nipples hurt, they are so hard. See?" Carolyn raised her shirt to show her nips poked out like pencil erasers.

Which, of course, made Myra and the other girl, Debra, do the same. They all had erect nipples and were squeezing their thighs together.

The dude, Joey, was still buzzing hard from the blast, his eyes fixed on the titties like he was hypnotized.

When I looked at Vic, that crazy muthafucka was locked onto Carolyn's breasts like a missile. I nudged him and shook my head. I noticed, too, but I wasn't suicidal.

While they came down a little, I dropped the ounce

with the sixteenth cut back in the cooker, and added another sixteenth. I weighed out two more and hit them with an eighth each. I dropped the four ounces with the eight ball cut into separate plastic bags.

By now, the last hit had worn off enough that the four smokers were ready for their next hit. I cut hits smaller than the ones before off the last ounce, the one with the quarter cut. I already knew the amount of synthetic I wanted to add to the dope, but I needed to know what would happen if I added a little more.

All four were in their stride now, and the crackle of the dope sounded like popcorn. Joey was the first to break. He ran out the back door. When I followed, he was throwing up beside the house. As I approached him, I thought I smelled shit.

I stepped back inside and saw the girls all in a daze. I followed Vic's eyes and noticed that Myra's pants were wet in the front, like she had pissed herself. When she stroked the front of her crotch with the tip of the pipe, I knew that wasn't it.

Debra just said, "Fuck it," and jammed her hand down the front of her pants and finished herself off. Breathless, she looked up at me. "The last time I did a shot of coke and it made me come, we were spiking it. That shit is the bomb."

Carolyn reached for the front of Vic's pants.

I grabbed her arm. "Wait. We got to go take care of some business. Y'all can play around later. Here." I gave each of the girls a baggie.

I stepped to the door and called Joey to give him his.

I told them some of the good shit would be on Bethune in a couple of days. Then I ran them off.

"Shit, cuz. You see that? That last batch is the one. Man, ain't no way we can sell that shit. It's too good. Them hoes are pros, and if it did them like that, it might kill some weak-ass smoker."

"You probably right."

"Them *O-Z*'s looked kind of small, though."

"They were. I cooked it all the way, so we lost a lot of weight. There are two ways to fix that. One, we can put in the synthetic and put a whip on it, or we could use procaine or lidocaine along with the good shit, and keep the weight up."

"Your daddy was the baller. You know more about that shit than I do."

"Okay. Let's pack all this shit up, go by the head shop and buy some good cut, then back to the condo to turn fifty birds of bullshit into fifty of gold."

Now I had all the tools, over sixty kilos of the best product in town, with an almost unending supply. I could take any bullshit, dirt-cheap dope and turn it into the bomb.

I had my crew, and my first two legitimate businesses. I had weapons, and boys who were not afraid to use them. Most of all, I had Jas. Down with a nigger all the way, and all that to boot. What could stop me from becoming the king of crack in The Four-Four? Nothing. And nothing would.

I told you I wasn't a gangsta, that my life was laid-back and kind of square, compared to some of the other hustlers. I was about to find out I'd been lying to myself. I took to the game like a fish to water. I killed like an assassin, stole like a master thief, and I wore bling like a rap star. I had the best. I had it all. Was it worth the price? I'll tell you what happened, and you decide.

Part II

Chapter Twenty-three

Eighteen Months Later . . .

I pulled into the detail shop and parked in front of the small office. My Escalade was immaculate, as always, but I wasn't here for the service.

Before I could open the driver's door, Frank Collier came out of the busy shop area. "Yo, Chris! What's real, my nigga?"

"Just cruisin' an' blowing this killer."

"I was just about to call you. I know you won't believe it, but I'm just about out. Shit is jumpin' around here."

"No problem, fam. Just keep on doin' you. Get with my cousin and tell him I said hook you up. You want the same as last time?"

"Yeah, ten."

"Tell him to give you twelve, and knock off two points."

"Good lookin' out. Everything goin' smooth?"

"You know it. I gotta bounce. A few more stops, and I got a booty call to make."

"Yo, later, *C*."

I got back in my vehicle and drove off. I fired up the weed and popped in Lil' Mario's new CD and cruised back up Wilburforce toward Carver Road. My homeboy from Garden City was blasting, the weed was fire, and all was right with my world.

I dialed my cell and waited for Vic to pick up. "Slick, it's me. Where you at?"

"Over by Chenise's house."

"Well, pull it out and pack it in. You got business. I got a few stops to make, an' you need to holler at FC. I'll set things up while I'm out, and you do the rest. Feel me?"

"Got you, cuz." His voice got lower. "Jas gonna cut yo' piece off, you don't be careful."

"I got this, cuz. Just watch my back."

"Always. I'll tell her you busy with José."

"How's Chenise?"

"We cool. You know how it goes."

"Well, be easy, Slick. Later."

It would take me another hour or so to make my rounds. Frank Collier's detail shop was my first stop. His brother's place on De Soto sold wheels, Boar Hog and Lucille ran a barbecue place on Little York a few blocks from their house, and my other lieutenants had different businesses all over the hood.

The whole hood, Acres Home, was mine, as far as

crack was concerned. I was the king of the dope dealers. The Cake Man. My achievements in the last eighteen months had exceeded my wildest expectations. Everybody got paid.

Of course, I had help. Boar Hog, both Colliers, Fred Jackson, his cousin Moochie, and young Trey from The Corner were my main men. Vic was pretty much over them. Jas did such a good job of washing the money through all the legit businesses that I really wasn't aware of how much legal cash I had.

Because of the way I set everything up, following my Daddy's advice, we could spend the money, or a lot of it anyway, without attracting the attention of the narcs. So not all of them were on the payroll.

Jasmine was my woman. We hadn't made it official yet, but it was only a matter of time. She was the one I trusted with everything I was, as well as everything I had. Our thing was a done deal, as far as I was concerned, so naturally I made the same mistake as most men. I took her for granted.

She and Momma had opened the hair salon and nail shop like they'd planned. It was a huge success. The place would have generated a nice income even without the massive amounts of cash my dealing injected daily. Jas was even taking evening courses at U of H.

Vic would follow my route in a few hours and pick up cash from each spot. He would deliver it to Jas or Mama through the rear of the shop. During the remodeling process, I'd had a huge, concealed underground safe installed. Only four people knew about it: Me, Jas, my mother, and Vic. Jas kept track of how much and where it was washed.

I had the Escalade and a Jag. Jas had a Benz and a 'Vette. Our new house off T. C. Jester on a two-acre wooded lot was really nice, but not a mansion. What's more, our supposed incomes barely covered the mortgage and car notes. We looked good on paper.

Like I said, I was all that. I'd hired the most expensive lawyer in Houston to take over Big George's appeal. Another couple of years, and me and Jas could buy our own island if we wanted. Nothing and no one could touch me. My soldiers were legion, and well-armed. They would die to protect the life I'd made possible for them.

Even the cops appreciated my flow. After the months of violence that went along with my come-up, the neighborhood was quiet and safer, since no one challenged my empire. You could make more money doing business with me.

Keeping a low profile was damn near impossible. The dope game was the biggest source of income in the hood, so I became visible in a constructive way. I gave back to the hood. Me and my crew helped the elderly with food and finances. We re-built the community center on Bland. And we bought new goals and playground equipment for four neighborhood parks. You could say I was the unofficial mayor of The Four-Four.

My wardrobe was tight. SJ, Dino, Armani, and every high-end brand name filled my closets. Jasmine's closets were even heavier, and her jewelry could have funded a small country's deficit. We were so busy coming up, we hardly had time to flash.

It was only natural that as I drove through the streets that people from all walks of life wanted to get at me. Though very young (my twenty-first birthday was only two weeks earlier) I had shown myself to be as acute as many older heads.

I had bodied more than my share of men. The thing the players admired most was that I'd done this not only in a short period of time, but without going to jail or shedding my own blood. Shit, I bought into the hype so deeply and completely that I even began to think I was bulletproof. Right.

Chapter Twenty-four

I finished my rounds with Trey and the youngsters over on Mayview. Of course, I had saved the best for last. Boar Hog still ran the area around his house. Part of his domain was a dope house near the end of Covington, which this young hustler named Derrick ran for him.

Earlier, I had called Boar and "volunteered" to pick up his take from the kid. There was hesitation in the old dude's voice when he accepted, and I knew what that was about. He knew what my motivation was. Normally he wouldn't give a shit, but me, him, and Jas had been there at the start, and he felt for her. He wasn't about to get in mine, though.

Derrick's sister, Talisha, was the reason behind my altruistic act. The girl had just gotten out of TDC and was jailhouse thick. Standing 5-5 or so, she was a pretty redbone. What stopped traffic was that ass. Very few women

I had seen, including those honeys on BET, could hang with my Jas, who was the complete package, and Tally was no exception. But this sister had a way of walking that had each ass cheek moving in opposite directions, and independent of the other.

Boar Hog's cell phone battery had gone dead a week ago, and I had taken the call from Derrick. He had a pretty big sale lined up, so I dropped off a package for him. Tally came to the door wearing just a t-shirt. When she turned to walk away, I was sprung. When she looked over her shoulder and saw the tent in my sweats, she gave me a wicked smile.

I'd made arrangements to drop by today with her brother. He knew the deal and was cool with it. I sensed his sister's hand in his cooperation.

Derrick opened the door for me and jerked his thumb toward the rear of the house. In addition to the house we were in, they had a small one-bedroom hut built in the backyard that was normally used by an older brother who was doing time. That's where Tally waited for me.

She stood in the doorway of the little house waiting for me. All she had on was a long Rockets t-shirt. The light from the room behind her backlit her, so I could see that she had nothing on beneath it. The sight of her thick bush and firm thighs silhouetted through the shirt made me instantly hard.

As I approached the door, she turned and walked into the room behind her. *That ass!* I was inflamed with lust.

An image of Jas flitted across my mind, but I pushed

it away. Lately, it was becoming easier and easier to be unfaithful, just as it was for me to buy clothes, shoes, bling, and other shit I didn't need and rarely used. Without even realizing it, I was completely caught up in the game and all that went with it.

Banging the door open, I caught Tally from behind. I reached around and cupped her tits and reveled in the sensation of that luscious ass pressing into my crotch.

She twisted around to face me. "I've been wanting to do this for a long time," she said. Smiling hugely, she dropped to her knees and freed my dick. She flicked the tip with her tongue then sucked it into her mouth.

Four years in the pen obviously had her horny as hell. My dick felt like it was in a furnace.

I let her bob her head back and forth a few times, but I was too far-gone. When I pulled her head off me and raised her shirt, her thighs were glistening with the juice leaking from her pussy. Practically dragging her, I pulled her toward the little daybed in the corner. I spread her legs and started to push myself inside her. No sex in such a long time had her really tight.

"Oh! Oooh!" she yelled, as I worked to get all the way in.

Grabbing that big ass, I thrust hard. She threw her legs open wider, and I pushed all the way in. I felt the head of my dick bump her cervix, and she screamed. Her already tight pussy contracted around my dick like a vise. I pumped through her orgasm while she moaned and gasped.

When my dick popped out of her with an audible

sound, she raised her head. "Don't stop, Chris. Please, don't stop."

I reached behind me for my pants. "I've got to get a condom. Baby, you're the bomb."

"You don't need one. I can't get pregnant. I had an operation."

I didn't question her. By then, my dick was so hard, it hurt. "Get on your knees." I slid in until that ass stopped me. All day I had been dreaming about what it would feel like to fuck her from behind. My dick was jumping like it had a mind of its own. I knew I wouldn't last long, so immediately I started to fuck her long and deep, our bodies slapping together.

She grasped handfuls of the spread like she was trying to pull herself away from me, so I held her hips and increased the pace. When her pussy started to spasm this time, I was right with her, flooding her insides.

She pushed her ass back against my final thrusts. We remained locked together in passion for a minute then fell apart. No doubt about it, the girl's box was all that.

We fucked like rabbits for the rest of the night.

Just before dawn, I staggered to the shower while she lay comatose. Then I went home.

Jasmine was asleep in our bed when I got home. I couldn't stop the guilt this time. I slipped into bed without waking her. There was no way to rationalize what I had done. Tally was hot, but not only was Jas my girl, but she could top her on every level, including the sex.

When I woke up the next morning, she was gone.

I called her cell, and felt even more like shit when she babbled on about her classes, and how much she loved me. I hung up with a strange sense of foreboding.

Five o'clock that afternoon, I was in Lincoln City, my last stop before going home. I had promised myself that I would be there when Jasmine got there, even go to class with her if she let me. That guilt was a muthafucka. And it was about to get worse.

I was heading toward Victory on De Priest when my phone rang.

"What's up, cuz?"

I had known Vic all my life. I could tell by his tone that something was wrong. "What's the matter, Slick?" I was expecting to hear some drama about him and Chenise.

"About an hour ago, I was parked in front of CVS on West Montgomery. That fine-ass Talisha was there with some of her friends. The bitch was blowin' about how somebody had fucked the shit out of her last night, and how she was gonna make him her man. I'd just figured out she was talking about you, when I heard rubber burning. It was Jas' 'Vette hooking a U and jumping the curb. She bailed out waving her 9 and stepped straight to old girl. Chenise was right behind her. Jasmine pistol-whipped and stomped Tally like she was her momma.

"Nisa said that some girl had come to the shop talkin' 'bout how Tally was bragging all over the hood about how her pussy was so good that she took Jas' man. Jas said to tell you that you was a no-good dog an' she was through. You better go talk to her, cuz. She wasn't tryin' to hear me. Just don't get your ass shot off."

"SHIT! Where did she go?"

"I don't know. Nisa said she'd call me later. You fucked up, boy. For real, though, was Tally's pussy all that?"

I hung up on him and hauled ass. I knew I was in big trouble with my woman. The only thing I could think of right then was to find her and do whatever it took to make it right.

Chapter Twenty-five

When I pulled into our driveway, I saw the Corvette. Before I could get my hopes up, I noticed that the Benz was gone. She'd been here.

Jasmine wasn't answering her cell, so I decided to go in and wait. All the way here, I had been trying to figure out how to play this. A nigga could go hard and go, "My way or the highway," but that would only end up with her gone for good. No sense frontin' off some bullshit. I owed her better than that. This wasn't just some temporary piece of ass. This was Jas.

I'd shook my head at too many niggas who had lost good women, fucking around with one-night hoochies. Now look at me. The only way to play it was to man up, and hope like hell she was in a forgiving mood. My plan was to leave another message on her voice mail and wait.

I pulled off the envelope stuck to the front door and went inside. I poured myself a glass of yak (cognac) and sat down to read the note.

Chris,

I am pissed as hell, but my mind is already made up. I am gone. Don't look for me and don't try to call me. I need some time. By now you heard about me kicking that bitch Talisha's ass. It wasn't just because she fucked you – that took both of you – but because she disrespected me. I ain't no fool, Chris. I know you been fucking around even before this. I never threw it up at you because I didn't want to lose you. Back then I thought I knew you. Now I'm not so sure. We made promises to each other, and I kept mine. Nobody's touched me since we got together. Chris, who are you now? Do you know? I sure don't.

When we started this, you stole my heart. You weren't like the others, just out for a dollar. You were so real, so kind, so honest. Did the paper change all that? You don't even know anymore how much money we have. You don't know and lately don't seem to care what I do with it. The streets, the bling, the hoes is all you seem to care about now. I ain't gonna lie and say I don't love you no more, because I do. If you didn't want me no more, you should have told me. I don't even know if I want you. I don't know you. What I want is Chris – my

Chris. If you find him, bring him to me. If not, tell your Mama what you want me to do with your money. Have her put it in the shop safe, and I'll come by once a week to take care of it. You know I won't fuck you over. Think about what I said, baby. I'm not going to sit here and watch you destroy yourself and me too. I'm out.

Jasmine

I sat in a daze and read her letter over and over. Was I really that far-gone? She was right about so much, though. I had been knocking down a couple of fine young things. My old friend, Linda Olivares, this beautiful Colombian cousin of José's. And she knew! I thought I was being discreet, but that wasn't it. It was a shitty thing to do to her anyway, and not at all like me.

Maybe the enormous amounts of money had fucked me up without me realizing it. I wouldn't be the first one. I thought I was stronger than that. Right about now, though, it looked like she was the strong one, and I was the one who had fallen weak.

She was right about something else, too. I had stopped paying real close attention to what she did with the money. If someone under me was a dollar short, I knew it and collected. But whereas I used to help and direct her moves to store and clean the money up, but started leaving it up to her.

Jas wasn't a full-time student, but took business courses and real estate management seminars at the downtown campus. Her goal was to clean up all our money and get us out of the dope game. That used to be my goal too.

The money was safe. Vic, Boar, and the Colliers could run the streets for a while. I really needed to deal with what Jas had said. Who was I? And where was the real Chris? I had an idea how to find out.

I packed a few things and put them in the Escalade. A phone call let me know that my mother was still at the beauty shop. I drove over. When I walked in, she was alone.

Mama looked up when I walked in. "Boy, what the hell"—She stopped and just opened her arms to me.

I hugged her to me and we stood there for the longest. I let her go and handed her the letter.

When she finished reading, she said to me, "I talked to Jas. She does need a little space right now."

"I know, Mama. I do too. She's right. I don't know who I am or what I want anymore. I know how to find out, though."

"How?"

"I'm going to Roxie. Tell Jas I'll have an answer for her when I get back. Tell her I'm sorry, and no matter what, I love her too. I'm leaving tonight. Vic will take care of everything. I'll call you."

"Okay, baby. I think that might be best. Your daddy . . . never mind."

"What?"

"You go on. Get yourself together. We'll talk when you get back."

I hugged and kissed her. Then I left to find my cousin.

We met on Bethune, me, Boar, Frank, Freddie, and Vic, and two hours later, I was on the highway.

Chapter Twenty-six

After being gone for five weeks, I came back to a full-scale war. The events leading up to it were relayed to me later by my people. This is what happened.

Jasmine sat in the office behind the beauty shop. Miss Dorothy was in front handling the customers for both her shop and the nail shop next door. As hard as she tried to concentrate, Jas couldn't keep her mind on her record-keeping. Her heart and emotions were in turmoil. Part of her was still so pissed off at Chris that she was tempted to go out and get some dick, just to show him that two could play the game. Her predominant emotion was hurt, though. She truly loved the asshole. How could he do this to her? To them?

When a woman stepped out on her man, the guy was

fixated on the physical act of cheating. Some other man had touched, held, kissed, and dug all up in what was supposed to be his. With women it was different. The physical act of what her man had done paled beside the fact that he held her feelings and her person in such low esteem.

It was important that her man understand her, and respect all that she gave to him. How she always put his wants and needs first and gave him not just her body, but everything else that she was. She wondered what to do.

Jas had allowed herself to believe that he was different. That he was the one-in-a-million man truly worthy of all her love. She'd decided early in life that she wasn't going to settle for the mold her birth and background dictated that she adhere to, using her body to play some dopeboy out of money, clothes, jewelry, and other material possessions. She knew that she was fine and beautiful, but she also knew she had a sound mind as well, so being just another hood ho wasn't an option for her.

Then, just as she had mapped out her plan—college and hard work until she could start a career—along came Chris. Her attraction to him had started when they were kids. He seemed so different, so far removed from the street hustler's life.

Everybody knew what his daddy did for a living, but it seemed to have no effect on him. Then came Herman. She knew that Chris had been forced into the game, and she also knew the risk she was taking when she tried to help him.

That night at her aunt's, when she realized that he'd almost been killed, something changed in her. She knew then that he was the one. There was nothing she wouldn't do to have him, to help him, and to keep him.

Well, the first two were a done deal. The last was up in the air. If he was just going to treat her like a piece of meat, then she might as well act like one. Fuck! Who was she kidding? That just wasn't her nature.

She had enough money now to do whatever the hell she wanted to with her life. And what she wanted to was to have this nigga's babies and to spend her life with him. But first she had to get his heart right and adjust his attitude. And she was just the bitch to do it.

Jasmine sat back and relaxed. This was a decision she could live with. She had never been a quitter, and wasn't about to start now. Chris' ass was grass, and she was a John Deere tractor.

She picked up the phone and dialed. "Hey, Vic."

"Jas! What's up, baby? You need anything? Chenise just went to get us something to eat."

"I didn't call to talk to my sister. I wanted to ask you a favor."

"Anything you need."

"I'm not trying to put you in this mess between me and your cousin, but I do need to know something."

"What?"

"Vic, do you think Chris really loves me?"

"I don't mind answering that question at all. I know he does. You're the best thing that ever happened to him. And I'm in a position to know."

"Then why?"

" 'Cause he, like me and the rest of the male half of the species, has two brains. The one below our belts is much smaller, but most of the time it's the strongest. And the pressure on him was hard."

"I don't know what I'm going to do, what's going to happen between us. His mama said he was going to go try and get himself together. I can respect that. When you hear from him, tell him we'll talk when he gets back. For right now, I need space as much as he does.

"By the way, Chenise dropped off the flyers for your opening. I'm going to put them up when I get through with the books. I'll be there with bells on."

"Okay, Jas. I'll tell Chris what you said. Bye."

Jasmine hung up the phone with a smile of satisfaction. Her message through his cousin should put just enough pressure and induce just enough doubt so that Chris would come on with the real. Besides, it had been his mom's idea.

Now that her mind was settled, she made short work of her calculations. Being practical, she had done a firm estimate of just how much money she and Chris had. Even she was shocked at the amount. It was past time for them to start doing something else. Before it was too late.

Vic, Boar Hog, the Collier brothers, and the Jackson's

all had businesses in the neighborhood that helped clean up their money. It justified their homes, cars, clothes, and jewelry, but short of taking over a Fortune 500 company, there was no way to clean all the money as fast as they were making it.

Jas was learning things in business school that would help, but her and Chris, Vic and Chenise, and Miss Dorothy were the only ones whose money she would directly control. The nightclub that Vic was going to open in about a month would help.

Behind the strip center where the beauty and nail shops sat was a large apartment complex that could have well passed for projects. Trey-Deuce ran the dope sales there for Chris.

The youngster had come up. His family was financially secure for the first time. And he didn't play much basketball anymore, since he was too busy running his little fiefdom and stacking paper.

When Chris' woman came through passing out flyers promoting the opening of a new club over on I-45, Trey and a couple of his crew followed behind her to help out. Trey worshipped Chris, and nobody was going to bother Jas while he was around.

When they were done inside the apartment complex and stepped back through the hole in the fence that separated it from the strip center, Trey frowned at the gold Benz parked in front of gas pumps of the convenience store. Three 6 Mafia's "Doe Boy Fresh" blasted from the interior, but Trey couldn't see if anyone was inside the car.

When Jas walked by on her way to the nail shop, the driver's door opened. The rap music died, and there was a long, shrill whistle.

"Shit! Shorty, you just got to holla at a brotha. You the hottest thang in H-town."

Trey knew the speaker was Ali from Studewood. The nigga had paper, and he ran the whole neighborhood from Crosstimbers to The Loop, and from N. Shepherd to the 45 freeway. The boy had a reputation. He'd take your money, your pussy, or your life, if you crossed him.

Trey whispered into one of his soldier's ear, and the kid took off.

"Hey! Hey! Don't you hear me talkin' to you?"

Jasmine turned to face the car. "Are you talking to me? 'Cause if you are, the name ain't *Shorty*, and it ain't *Hey*! I appreciate the compliment, but I have to tell you that I'm taken."

"Whoever the lucky boy is, he can't possibly do the things for you that I could."

"Brother, that's twice you've insulted me in one day. What makes you assume that I need any man to do anything for me? And if I do, I've got my own personal King. Chris King."

As she turned to continue on her way, Ali's eyes locked on her ass. *Chris King*. He'd heard of the young nigger. Had this hood on lock. Maybe he had to join his daddy. Well, Ali had a hood of his own, and this bitch was just too fine to let get away.

When Jas heard the footsteps behind her she turned.

Ali froze as he heard a series of clicks. The first came from the 9 the fine-ass bitch had pointed at his face. The rest came from the six youngsters that surrounded him. They had come from nowhere.

"Say, playa, the lady don't want to be bothered. You got a problem with that?"

Ali was seething inside, but he was no fool. The woman looked like she'd be the first one to bust a cap. "No problem, man. No problem."

When his boy walked out of the store, Ali turned and went back to the car.

Jasmine stood within the circle of guys and watched the Benz peel out of the parking lot and head up Little York toward the freeway.

"That bitch and them little niggers gon' pay for that shit. You know those boys? The bitch is King's girl."

"Naw, but I know where we can find them in a few weeks." He held up one of the flyers Jas had left in the store.

Chapter Twenty-seven

On the northbound side of Interstate 45, between the Crosstimbers and Tidwell exits, sat the shopping center that contained Vic's new nightclub. RUMPSHAKERS was opening tonight, and it promised to be hugely successful.

Vic had spared no expense in re-modeling the two-story building that used to be a furniture store. Twin bars ran along two walls of the deep building, and stopped twenty feet shy of the rear wall, where the stage with state-of-the-art sound equipment was set up. The circular dance floor took up most of the center, while small tables and counters filled every nook and cranny. A set of stairs rose from the north end of the floor near the entrance, and led upstairs to the VIP section of the club, where the seating was reserved, and a balcony overlooked the stage below. Vic and Chenise's offices were located upstairs also.

Angry voices were coming from behind his door.

"I still don't understand why that bitch had to be all up in your chest like that. If a nigga was sweating me like that, you would be ready to start some shit."

"Chill, ma. You know she was just trying to get me to go with her cleaning service."

"Bullshit! Don't play me, Vic. I love yo' no-good ass, but don't get it twisted."

"No. Don't you get it twisted, baby. Ain't you the one who said that we were just going to be together when we could with no strings attached?"

"Yeah. And where were you when we both decided that we wanted to see if we could make it work just between us? It was your idea, I think."

"Well, it seemed like a good idea at the time."

The minute the words were out of his mouth, Vic knew he had fucked up.

Chenise's face grew red. "Seemed like? Seemed like? Well, I tell you what—FUCK YOU!"

He called out to her as she slammed the door behind her. Frustrated, he swiped his hand across the desk, knocking a pile of paper and other objects to the floor. Shit! He didn't need this headache right now.

Problem was, he had been feeling that freak Brandy. Bitch was all that while she was trying to sell him on her uncle's cleaning service. Just because he was in a relationship with Chenise didn't mean he was dead, did it? It's not like he was planning on doing anything. He'd have to straighten out things with Chenise later.

The band was set up, the emcee was ready, and he had actually gotten the Colliers to holler at their homeboy, Chamillionaire, and convince him to spend a little time on stage. The house would be rockin'.

Chenise sat in one of the private rooms upstairs and drank her third glass of cognac from the room's stock. She'd forgotten who had the room for the opening, some drug boy, and she really didn't give a shit. After all, she was part-owner of the club.

That fuckin' Vic. Acting like she was supposed to just sit back while he let some big-tittie ho rub on him like a puppy. He had her fucked up! Nice was for Jas. And look where it had gotten her. Them King men had life and bullshit mixed up.

So deeply was she involved in her thoughts, Chenise didn't realize that someone was beating on the door to the room for some time. She got up to open it and saw seven or eight people standing there.

The tall guy with the sparkling grille spoke: "We had this room reserved. There must be some kind of mis. . . "

"Hi! I'm Chenise Hughes, one of the club's owners. Your room is ready for you."

"Don't you remember me?"

"No. Should I?"

"I guess you pull heat on niggas all the time?"

Chenise was puzzled. What was this nigga talkin' about?

"Only when they need it. Y'all have a good time."

The man grabbed her hand. "Thank you, Ms. Chenise. We, or at least I would have a much better time if you would join me. My name is Ali."

"I have to go right now, Ali. Maybe I could check on you later."

"I'll look forward to it. Please tell me you're not married."

Chenise looked up at Ali. He was handsome in a rough sort of way, and the grille, the clothes, and the bling showed he had paper. Being slightly drunk and pissed at Vic, she made the worst decision of her life.

"No. I'm not married, and to tell the truth, I'm not sure if I'm even in a relationship."

This was all Ali could hope to hear. The fine, beautiful bitch that had dissed him in a parking lot a month ago was singing a different tune tonight. Yeah. He owed her. And when he got through with her, he'd pay her little crew a visit.

"Then by all means, let me invite you to spend the night with us. We can dance, drink, and I've got some killer weed if you're so inclined."

"I don't know about the night, Ali, but I promise I'll be back shortly to join you for a drink and a dance. Bye!"

As Chenise walked away, she realized she'd made a promise that she wasn't at all sure she wanted to keep. There was something about Ali that she didn't trust. He was good-looking enough, and obviously had money, but something wasn't right. Besides, though she was still a little pissed off at Vic, that's who she wanted to see right now.

Chenise greeted the ballers and big spenders in the VIP section as she made her way to the stairs. She knew that Vic would be at the door. Actually, she was supposed to be with him.

"Man, I don't care what nobody says. That bitch Chenise is fine!" Chino stood at the railing overlooking the dance floor. "Somehow, her tits look bigger from up here."

"With an ass like that, I don' care if she ain't got no tits. An' I'm gonna be all up in it."

Ali and his boy Chino were watching Jas talking to the Colliers near the dance floor. They had no idea her and Chenise were two different people.

"I'll be back. I'm going to go get her. Make sure everything is ready."

When Chenise got to the bottom of the stairs, she turned toward the front door. Suddenly, she stopped in her tracks. Vic was standing there in his tux greeting the patrons, with that bitch Brandy right next to him in some shit that made her look damn near naked.

Her first thought was to snatch the bitch up and put her foot in her ass. Maybe she should go to her office and get her piece and pistol-whip her triflin' ass. Then she thought about her last conversation with Vic. Maybe this was what he wanted. He certainly looked happy enough.

Well, she wasn't chopped liver herself. In fact, there was a perfectly acceptable man waiting upstairs to show her a good time.

Fuck it. And him. And that bitch too. She retraced her steps and started back up the stairs.

Chapter Twenty-eight

For a while, it became like a comedy of errors. Jasmine, not really feeling like being out, had come only because of Vic and her sister. All the ballers and players in The Four-Four were there, as well as those from Third, Fourth, Fifth, and Sixth Wards, Kashmir, Settegast, Sunnyside, South Park, Greenspoint, Southwest, all the black neighborhoods in Houston. The place was filled to capacity and beyond. There were some nice clubs in town, but this one was off the chain.

As Jas danced with Vic, the Colliers, Trey, and even Boar Hog, Chenise strutted her stuff with Ali. It was a miracle that she and Ali didn't come face to face.

Vic wanted to teach Chenise a lesson, and she was likeminded. Brandy climbed Vic like a tree, while Chenise backed that big ass up on Ali on the dance floor. They were both acting like children. Unfortunately they were about to learn a very harsh lesson.

Jas was so caught up in her own misery that she really didn't notice what was going on. She hadn't even seen her sister to congratulate her. She did manage to track Vic down before she left at 1 a.m. She had to pick Miss Dorothy up in the morning, and she wanted to head home.

As she crossed the parking lot, she noticed a guy pause while getting into a gold Benz. He looked at her as if he'd seen a ghost. She didn't look directly at him, but put her hand on her pistol. The guy looked kind of familiar, but she knew she didn't know him. He looked almost Oriental.

Jas noticed that he drove around the building, instead of taking one of the lanes that would take him to the freeway feeder. She knew from her sister that there was a rear parking lot for the VIP rooms, which were accessible by an exterior stairway that led to a hallway behind the rooms. Since logic dictated that these expensive private rooms would normally be rented by young players, the private access was a perk.

Jas figured it was none of her business anyway. Maybe the dude was just admiring her. So she drove off.

"Hey, Ali! Man, how did you let her get"—Chino stopped in mid-sentence as he saw Chenise sitting on the VIP rooms sofa.

"Chino, what the fuck are you babblin' about?"

Leaning over Ali's shoulder and speaking in a whisper, Chino said, "I just saw what looked just like the broad Chenise getting into a red 'Vette."

"Well, you must be seeing things, 'cause she's right here."

"The girls are all gone. Let me know when you're ready."

Ali had sent their women home. Now only him, Chino, and Walt remained in the room with Chenise. He made sure that her glass remained full. When she made noises about it being time to go, Ali had signaled Chino to spike her last drink with roofies.

He turned back to Chenise. "Well, Ms. Hughes, I've had a wonderful time. Thank you very much. You may have had a little too much to drink, so I will help you get home." He stood and took her hand, lifting her onto her feet.

It was as easy as he'd known it would be to get her down the back hallway and into the rear of his Benz.

"You're sure you're taking me home?"

"Of course."

"Where's Vic?"

Who the fuck is Vic? Ali thought. "He said he would be right behind us. Don't worry."

Ali had done this enough that he knew Chenise, by the time he got her to Studewood, would be completely under the influence of the drug he'd slipped into one of her drinks. They didn't call it the date-rape drug for nothing. She'd be able to participate in her own rape, but wouldn't be able to stop it. And she wouldn't remember it.

On East Whitney Street, near Oxford in Studewood, sat a large apartment complex. The owner died, and his heirs and financiers were in litigation, and had been for years over who got what. The result was that the place was empty, since nobody was willing to invest the money in this high-crime area.

The 12-foot fence and NO TRESSPASSING signs meant nothing to Ali and his crew. They'd been doing business out of these buildings for the last few years. Chino lifted the wire they had permanently modified, so the Benz could drive through, and they took Chenise to the apartment they used for a fuck pad.

After helping her up the stairs and into the place, Ali dumped her on the king-sized bed and went to get ready. This consisted of snorting four huge lines of crystal meth. The high would last for hours. As far as he was concerned, the shit was the best aphrodisiac out there, except for maybe the roofies themselves.

When the speed slammed into Ali's system, he went into the bedroom and undressed Chenise. He looked down at her naked perfection and chuckled. He was about to fuck "the Crack King's" bitch. As often and any way he wanted to. He began to run his hands over her body, tweaking her nipples and massaging her ass cheeks.

Chenise, lost in the artificial bliss of the drug, began to respond, moaning when Ali bent to place his mouth on her pussy.

His grin widened as he continued to tongue her. When he judged her wet enough, he rammed himself into her. Her wet, tight, hot pussy felt like heaven. He fucked her steadily until he felt her tighten around him.

Ali wasn't interested in pleasing her. Far from it. He was a rapist. It was all about power, control, and pain for him.

He knew he had a few hours to kill before she would be aware enough to appreciate what he really wanted to do to her. To pass the time, he continued to pump into her while repeating her words to him in the parking lot. "Chris King's girl, huh? Didn't need anything from him, huh?"

The whole club saw how she was rubbing her ass against his crotch tonight. If she cried rape, he'd get her laughed out of court. His boys would swear she raped him. And right now, it was her come drenching the sheets.

Oh, this bitch was gonna pay. He started to slap her face as he drove himself into her. Now he was starting to get off.

Chapter Twenty-nine

Chenise woke to an insistent voice.

"Come on! Wake up! They may be back any minute. You've got to get out of here!"

She opened her eyes to see a face that was vaguely familiar. It was one of the women Ali had brought with him to the club. Her body was a mass of pain, and she could barely see out of one eye.

Briefly she wondered if she had been in a car wreck. Then her mind filled with flashing images: a fenced-in compound that looked like a prison; Ali helping her up a set of stairs; Ali undressing her; the rape; hands striking her over and over; Ali's friends all taking her at once, in her ass, pussy, and mouth; the pain.

"They—"

"Yeah, I know. That ain't all they're gonna do if you're still here when they get back. My ass will be grass too."

"Who . . ."

"My name is Helen. Let's get you out of here."

Chenise screamed when she tried to stand. When she turned her hazy eye back toward the bed, she almost vomited. The bedclothes were awash with blood and other fluids. She recognized what could only have been a couple of her teeth on the pillow.

"Jasmine," Chenise mumbled through her broken mouth. "Gotta call my sister."

"No time for that shit. I called you a cab. They'll take you to the hospital."

They made their way awkwardly and slowly out of the building, across the courtyard, and to the fence, Helen supporting Chenise all the way. The hard part was getting her through the hole Ali's crew had cut in the wire. As they stood beside E. Whitney Street, Helen could see a yellow cab approaching.

"Thank you."

"It's okay. Them niggas went too far this time. Dropping a roofie on somebody and taking the pussy is some low shit, but what they did to you is foul."

The cab driver balked when he saw Chenise's condition.

Helen raised hell and threatened to give his taxi number to the police, news stations, and anybody else who would like to know how he wouldn't help a dying woman.

He agreed, but only if she accompanied them to the hospital.

Helen hesitated. She knew if Ali came back while she was gone, he'd know who helped Chenise. To her credit, she only thought about it for a second before climbing into the backseat with Chenise. "LBJ. And please hurry."

Jasmine was dragged out of a deep sleep by the constant, annoying ringtone of her phone. Before she answered, she looked at her watch—6:45 a.m. *Damn*! "Hello?"

"Is this Jasmine?"

"Who wants to know? How did you get this number?"

"My name is Helen. I'm calling for your sister . . ."

"Chenise? What's wrong with her?" Jas was wide-awake now.

"Some guys drugged and raped her. They hurt her pretty bad. She's at LBJ. I brought her here and made the call for her, but I've got to go. They'll kill me if they find out I helped her. I'm leaving town now."

"Who? What guys raped her?"

"She'll tell you about it. I've gotta go. Bye." The line went dead.

In a panic, Jasmine threw on some clothes and jumped into her Corvette. As she flew down W. Little York toward the freeway, she left a message on Vic's voice mail to meet her at the county hospital.

Twenty minutes later, she was parking behind the emergency room of LBJ Hospital. *No way am I going to leave my sister here*, Jas thought as the doors automatically opened for her.

Ben Taub, and LBJ were the two huge county hospitals. They had bad reputations among the city's poor, which they didn't deserve. The time a person had to wait, even in the emergency room, usually ran to several hours.

As Jasmine walked to the service desk, she saw the wreckage of the underprivileged all around her. People sat with the same vacant stare one saw in jails and prisons. That look that said you were at the mercy of a system that gave less than a damn about you.

The truth was, Ben Taub, over in the Medical Center south of Downtown Houston, and her newer sister, LBJ, in North Houston, were among the nation's elite trauma centers. The number of poor needing medical assistance was so great that only the most serious cases, usually involving knife wounds, gunshots, or massive bleeding, got seen quickly.

After giving Chenise's name, Jas was told that she was in surgery, and that she needed to complete the admissions information, since the woman accompanying Chenise could not be found. The police had been called due to the nature of her injuries.

Forcing herself to calm down, Jasmine complied.

After providing the nurse with Chenise's full name, address, and place of employment, she was met by the emergency room doctor. The weary woman, looking much too young for such a high-octane career, gave Jas an overview of her sister's condition.

"She's got internal bleeding from what was obviously anal rape. Four teeth knocked out, two more broken, three broken ribs, contusions and scratches over most of her body, and a possible skull fracture. We managed to stop the vaginal bleeding.

"Ms. Hughes, this is one of the most brutal assaults I've ever seen, and I've seen plenty. The animals that did this should be punished. I had a rape kit run on her, and the evidence will be turned over to the police. She is in surgery now and, barring unforeseen consequences, she should survive. Physically, that is."

"Doctor, we can afford the very best of medical care. Should I have her moved, and if so, where?"

"For her immediate needs, she's in the best place she could be. You know that once she goes to recovery, her conditions won't be as comfortable as say Doctor's, St. Luke's, or Memorial. Let's just see how the surgery goes first. You can wait for her in the fifth-floor lounge."

Jasmine thanked the ER doctor and left. Before she took the elevators to the fifth floor, she stepped outside and called her mother's house. Then she tried Vic again. She wanted to call Chris, and knew Vic could contact his cousin, if anybody could.

Forty-five minutes later, Jasmine's mother rushed into the room. "How is she?"

"She's still in surgery. She's gonna be all right, Mama."

They hugged, and the tears fell from Miss Sharon's eyes like rain.

"I left *Q* and Yolanda with my sister. Oh baby, who would want to do this to her? I thought her and Vic was doing so good. He called me last night from the club looking for her. He said they'd had a fight and he didn't see her leave. Her purse and keys were still in her office. I thought he'd found her."

"Don't cry, Mama. Somebody drugged her and hurt her. They'll pay for that."

They were interrupted by a detective from HPD who wanted some background information on what had happened to Chenise. Jasmine and her mother repeated what they knew, including the fact that Helen was gone. The detective said he would talk to them after interviewing Chenise. Meanwhile, he'd send someone out to the club to start investigating.

Three hours later, Chenise was moved to the ICU. Jasmine had just finished filling a distraught Vic in on what she knew. The look in his eyes chilled her.

"It was some nigger named Ali. Runs most of the crack in Studewood. People saw her in and out of his VIP room all night. She was just trying to piss me off. That nigga is dead."

Chapter Thirty

When Jasmine left me, I knew I had fucked up. The words in her letter as well as the ones my mother left mostly unsaid affected me deeply. I guess you could say I was having an identity crisis. Who was I, really? I think I can honestly say that I didn't create the situation that turned me into a drug dealer and a killer. Certainly it wasn't the life my parents wanted for me, despite Big George's occupation.

The game simply was what it was. Like so many other young black men today, I just didn't see any other way to survive. Yeah, society would say that there is always a choice.

It's easy to say you've got choices when there is nobody's foot on your neck, when a whole society isn't designed to keep you and any other darker race at the bottom of the social ladder. Talk to an American Indian about choices, or a *barrio* Mexican. Go to the ghetto and explain how you can just choose your way off the bottom. Visit a prison.

So, no, I didn't beat myself up about my choice to take the conditions around me and turn them to my advantage. I wasn't some social crusader deploring the violence or debating the morality of the way I lived. I didn't decide that night in The Alley while I was dodging bullets that I would be the best doctor, or lawyer, or politician. My goal was to be the best dope dealer. And I succeeded beyond my wildest expectations.

In Acres Home, I was the King of Crack. The dope moved or stopped moving at my will. The women all wanted me, and the men envied me. For all practical purposes, my paper was unlimited. I had it all.

Then what the fuck was I doing way the fuck out in the country so far from civilization that I felt like I was in the Dark Ages? Roxie, located about twenty-five miles east of the river town of Natchez, is a small town in Mississippi of less than a thousand people. The mostly black population survives by farming or working in the few industries of the larger neighboring towns. It's the kind of place you have to be looking for to find.

During the six-hour drive through East Texas and across Louisiana, the only thing on my mind was Big Mama.

In the few weeks since I'd been here, I'd become convinced that the choice to seek her out was a wise one.

That's why Mama agreed so fast. She knew that if anyone could help me find myself again, it would be her own mother.

Big Mama was my grandmother. She was the one who taught me morality. Even more important, she was the one who taught me about love. By showing me. No one, not even my parents, not even Jas, could make feel surrounded by pure, unconditional, unquestioned love like Miss Mary Chambers.

My earliest memory is being smothered by her large, soft breasts as she hugged me. I can remember her teaching me my prayers at about five years old, rewarding me with a shiny coin when I got them right. Bible stories with Big Mama's own twist were my early bedtime stories.

Big Mama's house sat on a small hill amidst thirty acres of rich, black Mississippi farmland. The land was fallow now, the pine forest reclaiming it. My grandfather had died about ten years ago. When my granny refused to leave her home, Big George spent a whole shitload of money installing every creature comfort. And her grandchildren, children, and in-laws spent time with her and helped take care of the house, lawn, and small vegetable garden she kept.

My wish had been granted that first night I pulled the Escalade into her yard. She was alone. Our reunion was joyous. She was so happy to see me, and I felt free and safe the first time she wrapped her arms around me.

Of course, she fed me first with homemade biscuits so light and buttery, they seemed to melt in your mouth.

"Big Mama, does everybody in the family still show up at all kinds of hours for you to make biscuits for them?"

She laughed. "Of course they do, boy. An' I make 'em. You just ate six."

"I swear, your biscuits could cure anything. Just wait till Jas . . ."

My voice trailed off as I realized why I was sitting here.

"Help me put these dishes up, Chris. Then we'll sit on the porch and talk, like we used to."

When someone who was raised in a big city spends his first night in the country, there is always a sense of awe. The quiet can almost be felt. The stars shine clearly, and insects and small animals provide a pleasant background rustle.

I told her everything, holding nothing back. My original intention was to censor out some of the gory details, but just being in my grandmother's presence opened the floodgates. I also knew that her love for me was so complete that nothing I could ever say or do could ever change it.

She just sat quietly when I faltered in my recital. I got to how I hurt Jasmine, and her reaction to my cheating. I finished with a summary of all the things that had been going through my mind on my way down here.

Big Mama said nothing for a full three minutes after I stopped talking.

"Baby, you remember when I used to tell you Bible stories?"

"Yes, ma'am."

"Well, your favorite was stories about David. How he was minding his own business planning a future as a shepherd when he got picked to be the next king. He didn't seek or ask for the job, but when he saw he had it to do, he went at it. He killed Goliath, fought the king's enemies, and made a name for himself. Then, all those years the King tried to kill him, he did whatever he could to survive. He stole, lied, killed, and ran away when he had to. The old king died, and he ended up the undisputed boss. It was while he was on top that he made his biggest mistake.

"What he did was so bad that it pissed God off. He got punished. He had to pay the piper. His children hurt each other, killed one another, even tried to kill him. The rest of his life was mostly one big struggle. But somewhere along the way, in spite of all the bad things he'd done, all the mistakes he'd made, in spite of the fact that he had to keep paying for his sin, David remembered something. He remembered who he was. He remembered the things that had guided his heart when he was young. He was still strong, and he still stood up for what was his, but he did it now with compassion. He didn't let the same attitude that made God angry with him take over. He found himself and never let go again. Do you remember that story?"

"Yes, ma'am."

"Then think about it while you are in bed tonight."

Later, in my grandmother's guest bedroom, I reflected on what she was trying to tell me. She wanted me to see that I had somehow let my circumstances corrupt who I really was. The money, the power, the availability of the women had blinded me.

I remembered thinking that, when I could take care of Mama and make choices about my future, I would get out. That time had passed long ago.

Jasmine had been my rock, down with me for anything. She had given up all her plans and hitched her wagon to mine. It had never been her request that I be faithful, only that I be honest, trustworthy, and treat her with the respect she deserved. Lately, I hadn't done any of those things. If I lost her, it would be my fault.

Whatever happened between us, it was time that I started being Chris again. According to her letter, that was all she really wanted.

Thanks to Big Mama, I now knew what I had to do.

For the next few weeks, I got reacquainted with my roots. I fished and hunted with my cousins from Natchez. I did all kinds of chores around Big Mama's house. I ate until I felt pounds heavier. And Big Mama and I went on shopping trips to New Orleans.

Just when I finally decided I was ready to go home, I got a phone call from Vic. Trouble had come to my crew in a big way.

One of the facts that had always impressed itself on me about the Biblical kings was that they were always at war. Now I knew how they felt.

Before I could make lasting changes in how I was living, I knew that I had to make sure that the people who followed me were safe. I had to go to war.

Chapter Thirty-one

I got as much information from my cousin as he had available at the time. I knew Ali Hunter. I hadn't had any problems with him, and really didn't anticipate any. True, there was an old rivalry between brothers from his hood and mine that started way before we were born, but it had cooled down somewhat in more recent years. Now, it was a full-scale war.

Even if Ali hadn't touched one of my people, that shit he did was foul. Only the worst kind of bully and coward resorted to taking a woman's body by force. Ali had a reputation for doing that kind of shit. He had been locked up for it before, but none of the charges had stuck. He knew how to get away with it. He'd played himself this time, though, because there was gonna be hell to pay.

I gave Vic instructions on what to do in the hours it would take me to get back to Houston. He was hot as fish grease, but I convinced him that it was better to plan out how we were going to pay them back. I asked him to stay there with Chenise while I talked to Jas.

My heart was pounding in my chest when I made the call. I'd made up my mind what I wanted and how I was going to go about getting it. The circumstances weren't going to allow me to orchestrate the situation or to plan my comeback. This was business. Family business.

"Hey, it's me. How you holding up?"

"Hi. I'm hanging in there. It's bad. Real bad."

"I can't change what happened, baby, but I'm on my way. I'll take care of it."

"Thank you."

"C'mon, Jas, what's that shit? 'Thank you'? I know I fucked up, and if you dump me, I got no room to say shit, but me, you, Chenise, Vic, and the boys, we're family. You think 'cause you cut me loose that I won't be there for you? When were you going to call me? Or were you?"

I stopped talking. I literally held my breath waiting on her reply. I was getting pissed because I expected her to reach out to me automatically when she was hurt. Her failure to do so scared me. It made me wonder whether or not it was really too late.

She sighed deeply. "Chris, baby, who do you think I thought of first when I got that call? What was I supposed to do? We haven't spoken in over a month. Every day I have to stop myself from begging your mother or cousin to tell me where you are and how I can get in touch with you. For all I know, you were never coming back. Especially after what I said in my letter, every word of which I meant."

"Hold it, ma. This ain't the time or place. And it sure ain't the way I want to talk to you about this, but here it is—I fucked up. I let the money, the power, and the pussy get the best of me. I got lost. You didn't deserve the way I treated you. I don't deserve you. I'm sorry. My mother, my grandmother, and my own conscience are all telling me the same thing you did. And you're all right.

"Jasmine, I love you. Only you. There is nothing in this world I want more than you. Not the game, not the money, not the bitches. Only you. The choice as to what happens between us is yours, but right now I am coming home."

"Do you really mean all that?"

"Every word."

"Just come, baby, as quick as you can."

"Get in touch with Boar Hog, Trey, and Frank and Freddie. Tell them I said to lock and load. Meet me at our house tonight at ten. Tell Chenise I'm on the way. I'll stop there first. Now you tell me what happened."

"I think it may have been because of me."

Jas told me what had happened that day in front of the beauty shop, how she'd rejected Ali's advances and how she and Trey had run him off. She also mentioned that she'd told him I was her man.

"I think he got hold of the flyers I was passing out and decided to wait until the club's opening to teach me a lesson."

"And he mistook Chenise for you. Hell, I even did once myself. Any way you look at it, the asshole believed that he was pissing on me as well as you. It's not your fault, baby. It's his fake-ass gangster mentality. I'll show him gangsta. You just get as much information for me as you can. I don't want Vic to go off till it's time. My cell will be on. Keep me posted."

"First of all, we're gonna show him. And what do you mean, you once mistook Chenise for me?"

I told her about the morning in her mom's kitchen, and about how her sister threatened to tell her I tried to bend her over the sink.

Jas laughed. Then she got serious. "They really fucked her up, Chris."

"I'm—we're really going to fuck them up, baby. Bye."

After disconnecting the call, I went to talk to Big Mama. She understood, though she couldn't hide the worry in her face or voice. I hugged and kissed her goodbye, smiling at the thought of how she would fuss when she found the ten grand I left in her flour tin.

Thirty minutes later I was crossing the Mississippi River. I'd decided to go over to Alexandria, Louisiana, and catch Highway 171 South to Lake Charles. Then I could take I-10 over to Houston. That route would cut thirty or forty minutes off the trip.

Before I reached Jonesville, I had my mother on the phone. We talked until I reached Alexandria ninety minutes later. Mama told me she'd held the news about my father back until I could work out my situation. Neither her or Big George wanted me to make my decision based on what had happened.

The new lawyer had come through in a big way. He'd discovered a major discrepancy while reviewing the trial transcripts. My father's conviction was based solely on the testimony of two snitches. The narcs didn't find one ounce of dope either on him or in his possession. As fucked-up as it sounds, with the conspiracy laws being as they are, the government can convict you and sentence you to long prison terms with virtually no evidence.

The lawyer had discovered that the snitch wasn't even in Texas when he was supposed to have made large drug transactions with my father some five years earlier. The man was a guest of the Chicago police in the Cook County Jail at the time. That information was buried in the discovery documents, so it would be impossible to prove whether or not the U.S. Attorney's office had deliberately used illegal testimony to convict my father.

The fact remained, however, that the attempt by Daddy's first lawyer to impeach the snitch as a witness was improperly dismissed. The result was that a new hearing had been ordered in the Fifth Circuit Court of Appeals. My father would, in all likelihood, be free soon. Mama had been made aware of this weeks ago. All she had to do now was wait.

I was elated, but this still didn't change what I had to do.

I had decided to get out of the game, but what had

happened with Chenise had to be answered right now. On the streets, there was only one way to answer this kind of disrespect.

I caught my mother up on all the happenings with her family and reassured her that I was all right and there wouldn't be any more of my recent behavior that had worried her so much.

The rest of my trip was uneventful. I really pushed the Cadillac on those backwoods Louisiana roads, and by six o'clock that evening, I was entering Houston.

LBJ was my first stop. I flipped my phone closed as I exited on Lockwood, and by the time I had parked and gotten out of the SUV, Jasmine was cutting through the parked cars. She ran and threw herself into my arms.

As I lifted her off her feet in a hug, suddenly all was right again with my world. The troubles I had landed in the middle of seemed to recede. We couldn't stop kissing and touching each other. I swore then that only death would ever separate us again.

Chapter Thirty-two

My heart clenched when I saw Chenise lying in that bed, tubes hanging off her, monitors beeping the condition of her vitals. Even Jasmine's description of her injuries couldn't completely prepare me for the reality of her condition. Hot anger coursed through me as she looked wearily up at me and attempted a smile.

I knelt beside her bed and lay my head gently against her shoulder. "Don't talk, baby. It's gonna be all right. Me and your old man over there are gonna handle this." My eyes met Vic's, which were flaming with pain and remorse.

"Just relax and get well. You didn't do anything wrong. Me, Jas, and Vic are gonna be gone for a while, and Miss Sharon, Quinton, and Yo-Yo are gonna be right here until we get back. Everything's gonna be all right. Hurry up and get out of here so you can cook for me again. Your eggs are better than anybody's." I kissed her softly on the cheek and motioned for Vic and Jas to follow me out.

When I got to the waiting room, I sent Jas' mama, sister, and Q in to sit with Chenise. Then I turned to the others. "Did you take care of what we talked about?"

"Yeah, cuz. I want to kill those assholes real slow."

"Slow, quick, don't matter, as long as we take care of our business. Everybody will be at the house by ten. We'll set it up and handle it then."

Jas and I left Vic standing there staring out of the window, and we took my car back over to our house.

We only had a couple of hours before things would have to be set in motion, but what was next needed no discussion.

Taking my hand, my baby led me upstairs. She pulled me into the bathroom and started the shower, where we stood naked in the pounding spray and just held each other for the longest time.

I bent and kissed her soft lips, probing with my tongue, my hands roaming her perfect body. My dick throbbed against her stomach as our passion mounted. Her nipples felt like rocks against my chest.

Just when I thought I couldn't take anymore, she pulled away. Turning away from me, she placed her hands against the wall and bent over. "Now, Chris, baby. I can't wait!"

She didn't have to tell me twice. I stepped up close to her, my hard dick rubbing her ass, and bent my knees more as she placed me at her opening. I moaned as I slid into her warm wetness. I tried to take it slow, not wanting to hurt her.

She pushed hard back against me, wanting more. “Harder, baby. Fuck me hard!”

I grabbed her waist to steady her on the wet tiles and pushed myself into her hard. Losing myself to the sensation, I pounded into her.

Our position was awkward, and I couldn’t get myself fully into her. It seemed to be not enough for her as well because she suddenly stood, causing me to slip out of her.

“Fuck this,” she muttered. She ripped the shower stall door open.

Our bathroom was huge, with a big white rug in front of the triple sinks.

Jasmine knelt on the rug, her beautiful ass pointed up at me, and her glistening pussy pinkly shining beneath it. Her big breasts swung free.

I dropped down behind her and grabbed a double handful of her butt. When I pushed into her this time, I didn’t try to be gentle.

Jas had never been quite like this. It was new and exciting to me, and I was rapidly becoming hornier than she was.

I sank fully into her as she moaned and rotated her ass. We weren’t making love, we were fucking, pure and simple. Each time I withdrew my dick, I could see the thick, white cream of her juices coating me. I reached beneath her and cupped both hands on her shoulders, so she couldn't move, and slammed into her with short, brutal strokes.

Jas took it all, and pushed back for more. Suddenly her ass started to flex and tremble, and she emitted a keening sound and began to buck harder against me.

As her pussy seemed to melt around my dick, with a roar, I shot load after load of come into her. And we twisted frantically against each other for a while before collapsing on the rug.

Finally we were able to crawl back into the shower. A long, slow time of soaping and washing each other had us ready again.

This time we used the bed. Jasmine lay me down and proceeded to bathe me with her tongue. She wrapped her lips around the head of my dick and hollowed her jaws as she sucked hard. Then she licked the shaft and took my balls into her mouth.

I was clawing the sheets in ecstasy when she mounted me. She rode me, athletically raising and lowering herself, using her thigh muscles. Soon she was riding me hard.

When she started to come again, she pinched my nipples hard and brought me with her.

She lay on my chest as I stroked her back. She had never been this kind of aggressive during sex. I thought I knew what she was trying to say.

I told her, "It would have been easier if you had just heated up an iron and burnt your name into the dick."

"Yeah, but it wouldn't have been much fun. I just want you to know I can handle mine."

"You sure can, ma. Point taken."

She was still smiling as she drifted off.

The sound of the phone woke us up. I glanced at the clock as Jas reached for the receiver. It was 9:10.

"Hello? Helen?" Jas sat up, instantly wide-awake. "Where are you? . . . She'll live . . . She's in pretty bad shape . . . My man is here now . . . We're going to take care of it . . . Look, I appreciate what you did for my sister. If not for you, she'd be dead . . . When this is over, come back to town and call me. A job, house, car, whatever you need, we've got you . . . I know . . . We want to . . . His name is Chris . . . Yeah, that Chris . . . We could use the help . . . Conroe? . . . You got a cell phone? . . . Come now, and call us when you get close . . . Don't worry, he won't . . . Thanks. See you soon. Bye."

Jas hung up the phone with an elated smile. "Baby, that was Helen. She's the woman who got Chenise out of that place. She left town because she was scared of Ali, but she only went to Conroe. She will be here in about an hour. If we promise to protect her, she will help us get that bastard."

I knew this was a major break. I was gonna have Hunter's ass one way or another, but it would be a lot easier if I didn't have to shoot up half of Studewood.

I hugged Jas, and one thing led to another.

By the time we showered and dressed, Vic had let himself in downstairs.

I had just caught him up on the news about Helen

when Boar Hog and the Colliers arrived. Then Trey came a few minutes later.

Jasmine got drinks for everybody then took her position behind me.

I looked at my boys. "We've been through a lot of shit together. We started out with shit. We jacked dope houses, robbed pharmaceutical trucks, bodied a few knuckleheads, and built an empire out of nothing but our own blood, sweat, and balls. But we had more than balls. We had my baby, who can dance with any nigga here, we had Lucille, Carolyn and her sistas, and we had Chenise. I'd put our bitches up against any of them out there, and that includes most of the niggas.

"That pussy-ass nigga Ali from Studewood slipped a roofie to Chenise at the club, and him and his boys fucked her up. Raped her and damn near killed her. He thought she was Jas. Her and Trey had words with him a month or so back. He disrespected her and every one of us here.

"We been on top too long. Was a time not too long ago when a dime-ass nigga like that didn't have the balls to come into The Four-Four and try no shit. By now you figured out why we're here, if you didn't know already. We got to teach them assholes a lesson. Anybody got a problem with that?"

"Yeah, youngster—What we waitin' on?" Boar had been complaining for months that the game had got too tame.

Everybody laughed.

"This ain't the first time we had to tangle wit' that

nigga. 'Member a few years ago when yo' daddy's house on Yale got jacked? It was this same nigga. We took care of the problem, but him an' a couple of his boys got ghost an' I couldn't find them. Like I said, what we waitin' on?"

"We waitin' on this sista from Conroe. She was the one that got Chenise out of there. Used to hang at that apartment complex with one of his boys. She oughta be here in a short. She's gonna help us out."

Vic, his light-skinned face still flushed, seemed to regain control. The promise of action against those who'd hurt Chenise probably had a lot to do with it. He simply said, "Somebody help me get the hardware out of the truck."

Chapter Thirty-three

Jas covered the dining room table with a blanket. We hauled in the packages from my cousin's truck. The ones I was most interested in were the ones wrapped in oily paper surrounded by bubble wrap. While Boar and the Colliers were getting the last load, I looked at Vic.

"These the ones?" he asked me.

"Yeah. José was kind of hesitant to hook me up, but when I told him what had happened, and that it would eventually lead to a lot of increased business for him, he set up the buy."

I picked up one of the oblong bundles from the table. The packing grease was thin enough for me to make out the attachment for the grenade launcher. Boar said that a lot of the soldiers from the late sixties and early seventies abandoned the AR-15 assault rifle and its re-named clones, the M16 and M16 A series, for the Kalashnikov.

The old dude said he would much prefer the lighter M-16 in close combat, though they were prone to jam.

Close combat was what I anticipated, hence the grenade launchers. We had twenty of these weapons, plus our usual collection of shotguns and machine pistols.

Vic had contacted José as I'd told him to before I left Mississippi. I was pretty sure that he could get the armaments I wanted, and I was right. All those hours listening to Boar Hog's war stories had paid off. I didn't know how this shit was going to turn out, but I did know that the code I lived by, the one we all had embraced, demanded that I take immediate action.

Ali and his boys had better be ready, 'cause we were going to bring it in a big way. I wanted to ban Jas from the run, but there was no way she would go for that. I figured that out at Big Mama's house. The next best thing was to have the firepower odds stacked in our favor. Helen was another advantage I hadn't counted on.

Boar Hog stepped forward and took the rifle from my hand. "Look out, youngster. Let me show you how this works." The two missing fingers on his hand were no impediment as he quickly opened the bundle and began to assemble the gun. The old-school dude definitely appeared to be having some Vietnam-type flashbacks. A smile on his face, he cradled the assembled gun like it was a baby.

Boar Hog went through the ammo box and came up with what looked like a really big-ass revolver bullet.

"These are the grenades. Each gun will hold six of them. You load them like this"

"Damn!" Vic said. "Them don't look like the grenades they be throwing on TV."

"This ain't no TV show, youngblood. This gun will throw these things a couple hundred yards. You won't need that distance, though. Just be sure that when you select the grenade, you ain't standing next to what you are shooting at."

The M-16 looked like an over-and-under shotgun, the "over" barrel being real tiny, and the launcher looking like a big shotgun barrel.

Thirty minutes later, each of us was at least familiar with how to load and fire the thing.

Big George had left quite an arsenal to us anyway, and over the course of our come-up, we had all fired the AK's, AR's, and Uzis, sometimes for fun over at the dump, and sometimes for real as we took care of our business.

The anger at the Studewood crew had us ready to blast, but the sheer firepower we were wielding now had a sobering effect. Though Boar Hog was the old soldier, I already had an idea of how I wanted to proceed in taking down Ali.

"Boar, myself, Freddie, Frank, and Trey, we're gonna carry these launchers. Each of us will have three men with us. The dudes we want are gonna be in an empty apartment complex."

Frank asked, "You mean the one on Whitney just before you get to Oxford?"

"Yeah. We'll approach it from all directions. You'll turn off Crosstimbers by the Church's Chicken, and Trey, the next block over, which is Oxford. Freddie, come up Whitney from Yale. Boar and me will both come in the back. Each car will have one of these two-way radios in it. We'll do it right at the four a.m. shift change for the po-po. I've seen them hang around the N. Shepherd substation for twenty, thirty minutes."

"We're gonna be making a lot of noise. Laws are bound to show up."

"Freddie, if they do, they do. I'm hoping we can take care of business and fade. If not, then we play it by ear. I ain't tryin' to go down on no murder charge. These little bombs work on the cops just like they work on them niggas."

There. I had said it out loud. No matter what my soul-searching decisions at my grandmother's house had dictated, here was the reality. If you played the game, you had to be willing to play for keeps. Right now, it didn't get no more real than this.

I didn't think for a minute that we would be able to go to these dudes' turf, start a war, and all come out unscathed. We'd been lucky as well as careful up to now. It was time to pay up. When the game paid you, sooner or later you had to pay the game.

A real player didn't cry like a bitch when he got those lottery numbers in court. He didn't start snitching or cutting deals. When it was time to strap up and man up, he stepped up without hesitation.

Only a fool or a real loony muthafucka didn't get

scared, knowing he was going to be dodging bullets soon. Them muthafuckas ain't got no conscience and didn't care who they killed. Being a player meant you did what you had to, never mind being scared.

I looked over at Jas. Of course, she would be with me. I'd be lying if I said that I didn't wish that there was some way I could keep her out of this. But I can't deny being proud at the same time. This was a helluva woman, all the way down from the jump. Female or not, she was probably the coldest, most real player in the room.

My heart eased up a bit on its fear for her. We were in this together, just like always. We would ride together and maybe die together. Either way, we'd each be there for each other.

I was hit with remorse again for the way that I had let her down.

As if reading my mind, she came over to me and kissed me. "Me and you, baby," she whispered in my ear.

I was still answering questions, trying to see if I had missed anything, when there was a knock on the door.

It was Helen. I was surprised at how young she was. Shit, she looked about sixteen. No matter. She wasn't only the reason Chenise was still alive, she was also the only real edge we had in dealing with them niggas. Whatever, the slim, schoolgirl-looking woman was intelligent. Obviously, she'd been hanging around with Ali's crew for a while.

"The apartment complex is like a safehouse to them. Their dope and money are stashed there, but I don't know where. They don't sell out of there, but they run the hood from the building right behind the office. The whole upstairs is theirs. When you come off the stairs, Ali has the whole right-hand side. The door in the middle of the walkway is made out of steel. When it opens, there are only two rooms. The walls are gone from the neighboring apartments. A big-screen TV, PlayStation, bar, and exercise machines are all in the first room, along with the computer stand, sofas, and chairs. The other room is his playpen. A big bed, mirrors on the wall, posters of hip-hop honeys all over, this is where he fucks around.

"What he did to your girl was worse that what they usually do. When they want a woman, even if she comes with them willingly, it's always the same thing. Ali gets her high on some bomb-ass weed, and drops a roofie on her ass. Then him, Chino, Drake, and J-Boy all hit it. Sometimes there are others, but those four are gonna have her. When she wakes up, she don't remember all that happened, and Ali convinces her that she got high and went ho on them. He gives her a bunch of money, threatens her if he needs to, and kicks her out."

Her voice got low, and her light-skinned face flushed with embarrassment. "Sometimes they're so ashamed, weak, and broke, they hang around and hook up with one of the men. Your girl must have pissed him off. I heard Chino say that they had fucked up.

"They're gonna hang out at their base for a couple of days. Ali's people will be posted up on the streets around the complex. His business will be centered around the park until he thinks the heat has died down. He's more worried about what you'll do than the police. Just like you pay the cops over here, he drops out to the Studewood patrols."

I took her back over the setup again and again. She, as best she could, located the lookouts on the streets around the complex. Then I drew a plan of the apartments, and had her locate Chino's, Drake's, and Bolo's apartments.

By 2 a.m., we were ready. I felt better about our chances, now that we had really good intel. Every one of us had silenced 9's for the lookouts. All we had to do was wait for the shift change.

Chapter Thirty-four

The overwhelming influx of crack in the late '80s caused some serious logistics problems for the cops in Houston. Of its over 4.5 million metropolitan residents, about 25 percent are black, and another 25 percent Hispanic. The area of the city itself is almost 600 square miles (not including the extended metro area), compared to the 300 plus square miles of New York City. This meant that in quite a few neighborhoods the police force was poorly equipped to deal with the associated crime wave.

Houston's solution was to establish a series of police sub-stations in high-crime neighborhoods, a practice that had long ago been adopted by more densely populated cities.

With Jasmine riding shotgun, and Mouton, one of Trey's soldiers, in the backseat, I cruised up and down West Donovan, making a large circle down Shepherd and out West 43rd to Ella Boulevard, then north on Ella, and right on West Donovan, back to Shepherd. This allowed me to monitor the police sub-station on Shepherd without being obvious about it.

At 3:45 a.m., the activity in front of the station increased, patrol cars coming in from all over the area for shift change. It was time.

"Let's do it." I put the radio down and headed toward Studewood. I turned left from Shepherd onto Heidrich Street.

Jas checked her 9 and laid my M16 across her lap.

As I made the short dog leg on Old Yale onto Whitney, Jas whispered, "There he is." She pointed to a man in hooded sweats standing under a tree on the corner, the lookout on this end, just as Helen described it.

As I pulled over to the curb, Jasmine rolled down her window. "Hey," she said, "come here. I need a fifty pack."

Hearing a woman's voice say what he probably heard a hundred times a night, the kid visibly relaxed. "You gotta go to the park," he answered. "We're out up here."

"What?"

When he took a couple of steps forward, Jasmine shot him three times—*Phftt! Phftt! Phftt!*—and he went down.

I drove slowly onwards.

"Yo, cuz. Got mine." That was Vic. He had come up

Castor from Crosstimbers and taken out the lookout there.

Then Boar Hog checked in. "Young King, Harvard clear."

Then Trey. "Nobody on Oxford."

That worried me, since his street was one of the most obvious and direct approaches to the complex. I picked up my radio. "Circle around again and let me know. Everybody, hold a minute." I let the Yukon Trey's boys had stolen idle in the middle of Whitney.

Frank and Freddie both reported their lookouts down.

"He was taking a piss. He won't have to do that no more. Had a little bitty dick, too."

I smiled. "That's too much info, kid. Part two. Move."

The second part of my plan was simple. After making sure that the outer watchers were all taken care of, we would all exit the vehicles and come up on the complex from all directions. I thought there'd be lookouts close to the fence around the perimeter. If I was Ali, I would've had the place surrounded with layers of cover.

As I approached the front of the complex, Jas on my right and Mouton off to the left, I saw muzzle flashes.

Trey had taken care of the two men at the place where the fence was cut. When my group reached his, we all crouched down and waited. Boar Hog had the west side, me and Trey the south, Frank the east, and Freddie had the north. Within the next couple of minutes, they had all reported the fence clear. It had been only eight minutes since I had given the go signal.

Using a small penlight, it only took a few seconds for me to locate where the fence was cut to allow Ali and his people entry. All my people had big wire-cutters, and I waited until I had signals from each of them that they'd made holes in the fence.

"Okay, four. Slow and easy."

Everyone entered the complex from the four directions to converge as silently as possible on Ali's headquarters in the center. The rental office was before us. Directly behind it was the empty pool, and then the target building.

I whispered into my radio, "Okay, get ready for five."

To my way of thinking, it was a mistake by Ali not to have steel shutters, or at least burglar bars on the upstairs windows. He had a steel doorway installed at his place. Why skimp on the rest? His arrogance was going to be his undoing.

The final part of my plan was simple. From the east side and the west side, the Colliers were going to fire grenades into the windows, both Ali's and his henchmen's. Before they did that, me, Jas, Vic, Trey, and Boar would go up the north and south stairs to the second floor. When we heard the grenades, we would start our own assault. Everybody in the building died. Simple. In theory, anyway.

What fucked it up was that there was a guy in the pool. He obviously didn't see or hear our initial approach but heard something before I gave the final go, though. The burst from his AK cut down Mouton and one of the guys with Trey.

Somebody, Vic I think, fired a grenade into the pool. These shells exploded on contact. The shots from the pool stopped immediately after the explosion.

"GO! GO NOW!" I yelled into the radio. The timing was going to be fucked up.

When I got to the top of the stairs, I could hear explosions from the grenades being fired at the windows.

Within seconds, Trey had kicked in the nearest door to our left and fired a grenade shell into the apartment. The loud *WHOOMPH*! was followed by another as Boar did the one on the opposite end. Boar and Trey quickly did the other two doors. It was up to them to handle anyone left alive in those apartments.

Time seemed to slow down. I remember hoping that the kids assigned to bring the vehicles had done so.

Vic ran past the steel door and posted up ten feet down. Pressing Jas against the opposite wall, I nodded at him, and we both fired grenades at the steel door. The explosion was deafening in the enclosed space.

In his eagerness to get revenge for his girl, Vic fucked up. Instead of following the plan and blowing the hell out of Ali's place with the launchers, he burst through the door screaming as soon as the smoke cleared enough to see a hole where the door was. Then there was a hail of gunfire, and I saw him jerk a couple of times and fall.

I stepped into the door and triggered off three grenades in an arc. I heard bullets whizz by, and hoped Jas was still behind me. When I stepped back, I almost knocked her down.

Everything got quiet.

"Boar, help me get Vic out of here. He's hurt bad." I lay down my M-16 next to Vic. He had been hit at least twice, and there was blood everywhere. He was still breathing, and was moaning.

I looked up, and the room in front of me was completely destroyed.

I heard Jas on the radio telling everybody to get clear. She ordered the car to the foot of the stairs, while me and Boar lifted my cousin.

CRACK! CRACK-CRACK!

I whipped my head around. Somebody had come out from the bedroom through the smoke, and Jas had dropped her radio and blasted on them.

"That was that bastard, Ali," she said. "I got him. Let's go!"

As long as it seemed that we had been in there, only fourteen minutes had passed. We crashed through the cut in the fence and hauled ass over to N. Main. When we reached the North Loop, I told Trey to take a right and go to the emergency room at Northwest Memorial.

I told Pee-Wee, who, along with me, Jas, Boar, and Trey, was in the SUV, that he would have to stand up for us. Just before the turn into the hospital drive, I kissed my boy on the forehead, and me, Trey, Jas, and Boar got out.

We walked under the overpass to the Exxon station

and called Lucille to come get us. I wanted so bad to go with Vic, but knew that would be a mistake. The way we had assaulted that complex would get anybody the feds could prove was a participant a lot of years because of the weapons.

Pee-Wee would say that he was riding down Whitney looking for his crackhead girlfriend when this dude staggered out in front of his car, bleeding. That he loaded him up and took him to the hospital.

Vic would claim not to know who shot him or why, and the laws wouldn't be able to prove otherwise. What were they gonna do? Lock Vic up for getting shot? Our lawyers would chew them up. Arrest Pee-Wee for being a Good Samaritan? Same thing. What we couldn't afford was for any of the crew leaders to be caught up. We were likely to be on somebody's watchlist anyway.

When Lucille stopped gushing over the fact that Boar was in one piece, I had her drop us at my house.

We had lost three men, all of them Trey's boys. I called my aunt and had her go over to the hospital. She cussed me out, but she knew what to do. When Trey left, I sent all the weapons with him, except for the personal pistols belonging to me and Jas.

"That's it, baby," I said to Jas once we were alone.

"Yeah, we got to lay way low for a minute."

"That ain't what I meant—I'm through with the game. You too. It's time. I had already made up my mind, before I knew about Chenise."

"Chris, do you really mean that? Can you just walk away like that?"

"Watch me."

I took my woman upstairs and made her flush her pills. Then we started on the baby.

Chapter Thirty-five

An hour later, around six o'clock, Vic's mom called. He'd been hit in the left shoulder and in the thigh. He had a couple of surgeries in front of him, but he would live. The cops were buzzing around like flies. I gave her the lawyer's number and told her to get him up there now. Pee-Wee had made it out.

Jas got up to get ready to go see Chenise. She wanted to let her know her troubles with Ali were over, and to make arrangements for Chenise to be moved to the same hospital where Vic was.

I had just finished making us breakfast when the doorbell rang. Holding my 9 behind my back, I looked outside. It was my mother, with a huge smile. I let her in.

"Hey, baby. Where's Jasmine?"

I kissed her and called out for Jas. I figured the good news was about my father. "What's going on?"

Jasmine came down and hugged Mama. I shook my head at her. We weren't going to spoil her mood right now by telling her about Vic.

"I want both of you to sit down and wait for a few minutes. Then we'll go see your surprise."

A few minutes of half-heartedly trying to pry her secret out of her had us all laughing and in a playful mood. We were all in the kitchen when I heard the front door open.

"Get ready." Mama smiled.

"Yeah, get ready to die, muthafucka!"

Standing in the doorway with some other dude was Ali Hunter. He looked like shit, blood and brown shit covering his shirt and pants, but it was the big .45 in his hand that got my attention.

I glanced over to the counter where my pistol was, but knew I couldn't make it. Jas and Mama were both between me and the counter.

"You pussies thought you had me, huh? That was my house. I got a hundred ways out of there."

"What the fuck you want, man? You violated, and you know it. I did what I had to do."

"Bitch looks all right to me. Pussy was real good too. Look like she could stand a little more dick."

My anger flamed hot. Jas saw and tried to keep me from doing something stupid.

"Yo' dumb ass still ain't figured it out? That wasn't me. If you had stuck your rotten dick in me, I would probably shoot myself! That was my sister you drugged and raped."

"Wasn't much of a rape. She begged for this dick."

"Nigga, please. Everybody know last time somebody gave you some pussy was when your momma had you."

"Bitch!" He started to step forward.

The man with him grabbed his shoulder. "Ali, we got to get the cash to burn off. Let's just make homeboy drop out and get gone."

"Fuck that, Chino! We gon' get the cash. First, I'm gonna make him watch me fuck his girl, then his momma, if he don't drop out. If he's a good boy, I just might let him live. Come here, bitch."

"Stay where you are, Jas. Touch her, asshole, and you not only won't get a dime, but you don't get out of here either. Shoot me now, they can't get to the cash. You think I don't know you gonna kill us all the minute you get your money? Fuck you! I set off the alarm. Cops will be here in a minute.

"There's a way out, man. Let them go, an' I'll get you the money. No shit. The minute they drive off. How about it?"

I could see the fear, pain, and just plain hate working Ali's facial expression, but Chino looked like he really wanted to take me up on my offer.

Ali just twisted his face in a grimace of disgust. "Nigga, you still think you're the king of the hill, huh? Just like yo' daddy? Right now, from where I'm standing, you ain't shit. Think I'm dumb or somethin'? Well, smart guy, if you don't get that cash right now, the old bitch dies." He cocked the hammer of the .45.

I thought hard about trying to get to my gun. "Okay, okay, you got that. I just gotta go upstairs."

"There you go again. I ain't that stupid. Give my man Chino the combination to the safe. When he gets back, then we'll see what happens."

I didn't see where I had much choice. I told Chino how to find the safe hidden in the floor of our closet, and how to open it. There was about seventy grand in it. We didn't keep much money here.

When Chino walked out of the room, Ali turned to me. "Go over and stand next to your momma."

I did.

He then pointed the gun at Jasmine and started to undo his pants with his left hand. "You, miss high-saddity, too-good-for-a-nigga, come over here and suck my dick."

"Fuck you—Shit! Okay, just don't shoot me."

I looked over at Jas, shock on my face. *What the fuck?* She just smiled at me.

"Don't worry, daddy. I'm going to do him so good, he'll have to let us go." She opened her robe, and let it drop. She was naked beneath it.

Ali's eyes were buggin'. "Damn, it wasn't you. Your titties are bigger."

I finally snapped to the fact that Jas was using her head. If she could distract him long enough, I could make a play for my gun. Giving the maggot a blowjob was better than all of us dying.

I looked over at Mama, who hadn't said a word. She had the weirdest smile on her face. When I looked back at Ali, his eyes were still eating Jas up.

I saw a shadow move. Then Ali made a gurgling sound, and the arm holding the .45 went straight up in the air.

BOOM! The pistol went off, raining paint and plaster around us.

I dove for the countertop and my gun.

When I whirled to face the doorway again, I froze in shock. Ali's feet were kicking air a good six inches off the floor, one huge brown hand wrapped around the wrist holding his gun, another wrapped around his neck.

Muscles stood out in sharp relief, as an awesome strength held his weight one-handed. The hands belonged to my father, Big George.

With Ali's pants hanging off his ass down to mid-thigh, I stepped forward and drove my fist up between his legs as hard as I could. He couldn't say anything, but his eyes got wider. I took the .45 out of his hand.

Big George let Ali's feet down, placed both hands around his neck, and broke it like he was a small bird. At the cracking sound, Ali stained both ends of his boxers.

Suddenly the sound of a scuffle came from the front room then a sharp cry and a thump. Boar Hog stepped through the door.

I noticed the old goat's eyes get big as he peeped Jas putting her robe back on.

Daddy only had eyes for Mama. "You all right, Dot?"

Mama just ran across the room and threw herself into his arms.

I followed his example and pulled Jas to me.

"Your Mama told me about the trouble you had with

this piece of shit. They let me out this morning from the FDC downtown. I had told Dot not to let y'all know until I was sure. I went by Boar's to tell him to get you and Vic to wait a couple of days till I could check out the situation. He told me what happened, and we came over here."

"I'm glad you did, Daddy. Let me get this shitty-ass nigger and his homeboy taken care of."

Who could I call but Trey? That kid had damn sure proved himself to me.

Ten minutes after I flipped the phone closed, him and his boys were packing the bodies out.

Daddy took me aside and said, "Meet me at Boar Hog's in two hours," and without waiting for an answer, he took Mama's hand and left.

Epilogue

We sat in the darkness of the little neighborhood joint called CB's, the place where Jas had whipped Tally's ass. There was just me and my old man here now. Everyone who saw us came up to him and hollered. At Big George's request, the place had been cleared out.

I knew Daddy and Mama had been making up for lost time, but I pushed that thought out of my mind. Nobody wants to think about their parents fucking. Anyway, he had that "I-just-busted-three-or-four-nuts" look.

"Boy, I want you to know I'm real proud of you." Big George took a sip of beer. "When I went down, you stepped up and took care of business like a real man."

You've got no idea how good it made me feel to hear those words. I'd spent most of my life, it seemed, trying to win Big George's approval.

"You built a crew and an organization in damn near no

time that was bigger and better than the one it took me more than twenty-five years to build. That's good. It still don't change the fact, though, that I didn't want this kind of life for you.

"I got lucky, son. Real lucky. It ain't too often the feds get your ass and you wiggle out from under. I don't want to waste my blessing. The truth is, though, the streets are in my blood. I've been at the game so long that, in a way, I have become the game. I don't want to do nothing else. That's sad, but there it is. I don't think it's too late for you, though. I know you got paper. You also got a woman who's one in a million. I ain't gonna preach to you about what happened. That would be the pot calling the kettle black. But if you lose her, you won't find another like her.

"Chris, get out. Go to college, go buy an island, whatever you want to do. Take that girl and live. You ain't got nothin' to prove out here. You stood up then got down for yours. Niggas know you the King. No need to die trying to do what you've already done. Just remember, boy, whatever you decide, I'm with you. You're my son, an' I couldn't ask for any better."

Now, me and Big George had always been close. He had never been the kind of man to lay his feelings out there. For him to talk to me this way made me see that I had crossed some kind of threshold in my relationship with him.

"Daddy, I'd already made up my mind to do that. Me and Jas was talking about it just before Mama came over this morning. I know you said that I did good, but we both know that it was your connect, your stroke in the hood, that let me win like this. It's all yours, anyway. All I ask is that Vic, Boar, Trey, the Colliers, and Chenise be taken care of. I got a couple of jars of that pharmaceutical left, and you can have that too. Just be careful, and keep your head down."

He roared with laughter. "That's my boy! Now you lookin' out for the old man."

We spent another couple of hours there, catching up.

Three months later . . .

RUMPSHAKERS was jumping. Tonight was an invitation-only celebration.

Vic and Chenise were both out of the hospital and completely recovered. Also, me and Jasmine were going on a trip.

Hell, we didn't even know where we were going. Tomorrow morning we would board a plane for Hawaii, and from there we would go wherever whimsy took us. In addition to our marriage last month, we had a pregnancy to celebrate.

Vic and Chenise were making noise about making it official—At least Chenise was, and Boar was still dodging Lucille.

Nobody did any time behind the incident in Studewood, although Vic and Chenise were sweated about it for quite a while.

I think the police figured out that Ali and his boys had

drugged and raped Vic's woman, and he had elected for street justice. The sweating was for form only. They didn't give solving it their best effort.

Ali and Chino never did turn up.

There was some rumors about Ali's cousins from New York coming down to take over for him, but they didn't get here yet. I don't think they wanted any beef with The Four-Four, no matter where they're from.

Me, I just wanted to lay around in some tropical paradise and do all the fucking I could before Jas got too big. She said we could do it right up until just before she delivered, but I wasn't taking any chances. I wanted mine now.

I'm out. Peace!